Original frontispiece of the 1913 edition
published by Georg Müller, drawn by Alfred Kubin.

HASHISH

Oscar A. H. Schmitz

illustrated by Alfred Kubin

translated by W. C. Bamberger

afterword by James J. Conway

WAKEFIELD PRESS, CAMBRIDGE, MASSACHUSETTS

Originally published as *Haschisch: Erzählungen* (Frankfurt am Main: Südwestdeutscher Verlag, 1902)

This translation © 2018 Wakefield Press

Illustrations by Alfred Kubin © 2018 Eberhard Spangenberg / Artists Rights Society (ARS), New York/VG Bild-Kunst, Bonn.

Wakefield Press, P.O. Box 425645, Cambridge, MA 02142

This book was set in Garamond Premier Pro and Helvetica Neue Pro by Wakefield Press. Printed and bound by McNaughton & Gunn, Inc., in the United States of America.

ISBN: 978-1-939663-31-3

Available through D.A.P./Distributed Art Publishers
155 Sixth Avenue, 2nd Floor
New York, New York 10013
Tel: (212) 627-1999
Fax: (212) 627-9484

10 9 8 7 6 5 4 3 2 1

CONTENTS

TRANSLATOR'S INTRODUCTION

Oscar Adolf Hermann Schmitz was born 16 April 1873 in Homburg, the eldest of four children of an upper-middle-class family. His father was a high-ranking official who owned a railroad. The family relocated to Frankfurt when Schmitz was an adolescent. There he became such a discipline problem that he was asked to leave the Frankfurt Gymnasium, and finished up at the Gymnasium in Weilburg. After graduation, beginning in 1892, he studied economics, philosophy, and art history in Jura, Heidelberg, and Leipzig. At some point he also studied English. In this same period he traveled to Tuscany, where he met the writer Karl Wolfskehl who introduced him to the circle of aesthete poet Stefan George. Wolfskehl facilitated the publication, beginning in 1896, of some of Schmitz's Romantic and symbolist poetry in George's journal *Blätter für die Kunst*. Schmitz, however, soon had a falling out with George over Schmitz's criticism of painter and book artist Melchior Lechter, who frequently worked with George.

In 1894, Schmitz, having left university without a degree, began traveling—through Italy, and on to Budapest, Vienna, and Prague. He also studied art history in Rome. (In later years he also traveled to the Netherlands, Belgium, England, Ireland, and parts of Scandinavia.) Everywhere he went he sought out the local artists and writers. He returned to Munich to complete a law degree, but after the death of his father in 1895, he abandoned this pursuit. Living on his large inheritance, Schmitz began making a reputation for himself—as much for being a well-known dandy as for his writing—in bohemian and bourgeois circles. At times he temporarily shared living quarters with writer and translator Franz Hessel (the model for Jules in Henri-Pierre Roché's novel *Jules et Jim*) and with Fanny ("Franziska") zu Reventlow, the so-called Bohemian Countess of Schwabing (a bohemian and entertainment district in Munich).

Schmitz enjoyed the life of a literary dandy in Munich, but he was not overly impressed by the city itself. In his journal he wrote:

> In Munich one *must* come to the point where I am today: to a hypertrophy of cerebral activity. Munich is a city without much life, but with a great deal of artificial spirituality; no charming recreations, only debates in cafés, serious concerts, and the theatre. There are no truly tasteful musical-cafés, coffee houses, or cocottes. [. . .] Our imaginations, and our reminiscences of Vienna, Brussels, and Italy, have to help us along. Everything has to come from the imagination, from the mind. There are not enough peripheral excitements; in this there is something masturbatory.[1]

In another journal entry, he claims that the only reason he lives in cities is because of the women; otherwise he would live a hermit's life in the country.

Schmitz kept a journal for a little more than two decades. (Three volumes have been edited and published, spanning the years 1896–1918.) The entries make clear that Schmitz was a man who knew his own mind, a man of strong opinions, some of which could be off-putting. In his entry for 26 January 1898, he notes that an acquaintance has just offered to address him with the familiar *du*. Schmitz writes, "It has been many years since anyone has done this. No one dares because I appear cold and unloving." While Schmitz finds the man both clever and decent, he also finds him "tasteless and tactless." He doesn't record whether he accepted the offer of familiarity.

An earlier entry, for New Year's Eve 1896, details an encounter he had with an old classmate, now a boorish physician. Schmitz describes him as "lifeless [. . .] stereotypical and cruel," a man who dismissively discusses women in the open street. Taking off from this encounter, Schmitz writes:

One point at which most physicians fail is in regard to the abnormalities of more refined natures. For them, everything is equally morbid. For me, the *débauche mentale* is the ability to suppress everything sensuous from the sensual process, which can then, of course, lead to unprecedented excesses of imagination, without there being the slightest attempt at acting it out in reality, because of the stimuli that would then be added which act unpleasantly on the senses, as well as for the sake of certain inhibitory associations. Amorous writers are often chaste in life. Every perversity has one seductive basic idea. Each is a symbol of this idea. From cunnilingus to coprophagy: it's the idea of indulging oneself completely.[2]

In his journals, Schmitz freely intermixes records of the events of his days with more writerly concerns. Immediately above his account of his meeting the physician, he writes,

Since the time I found an artistic form, I have also had ideas I never had before.

And Schmitz worked a great number of disparate ideas in a number of forms. *Haschisch*, first published in 1902, was his second book. It was preceded in 1898 by the poetry collection *Orpheus*. Soon after *Haschisch*, Schmitz published *Halbmaske* (Halfmask), a miscellany of poems, sketches, and other writings. He also published fairy tales, novels that satirized bourgeois culture, a number of plays, a travel book, and several autobiographical works. In 1913, he published *Don Juan, Casanova und andere erotische Charaktere: Ein Versuch*, a nonfiction book about erotic characters from history. He wrote a number of popular books on politics, yoga, astrology, etiquette, and Jungian psychology. Schmitz knew this last subject very well: he underwent years of psychoanalysis, both Freudian and later Jungian. In December 1906, Schmitz together with Stefan Zweig attended a lecture in Vienna by Sigmund Freud, "Der Dichter und das Phantasieren" ("The Poet and Fantasizing")—after which Schmitz and Zweig went to a brothel.[3] In 1912, Schmitz first underwent analysis, which centered on his narcissism and his relationship with his highly successful father. Under the name "Patient B," he became one of the best known of the early analysands. In 2007, Schmitz was identified and his case made the subject of the essay "The Dark Side of a Dandy: The Writer Oscar A. H. Schmitz in Analysis with Karl Abraham."

The title has a double meaning, referring both to Schmitz's inner demons and to his light-shyness: during his sessions he asked to sit where his face would be turned away from the window.[4]

In addition to his popular books, Schmitz wrote reviews, essays, and more for magazines and newspapers. In part, this was prompted by economic necessity: he was married three times and later wrote that the financial fallout from his two early failed marriages (neither of which lasted longer than a year) forced him to accept any paying work. One of these pieces for hire was a review . of Sergei Eisenstein's 1925 film *Bronenosets Potyomkin* (*Battleship Potemkin*). Schmitz's review was a negative one. True to his feeling for radical individualism, he faulted *Potemkin* for featuring characters who were reduced to representing types, rather than construed as individuals: "Precisely the human, and thereby the artistic elements are fundamentally suppressed," he wrote. For Schmitz, the film was not a work of art; it didn't have enough humanity in it. This review prompted an aggressive response from Walter Benjamin, who defended it, largely on political grounds. In "Reply to Oscar A. H. Schmitz," Benjamin calls Schmitz a "cultural philistine," suggests he didn't even need to see the film to write such a review (and perhaps hadn't), and that his ideas were lazily taken from popular society novels. Benjamin faults Schmitz for not addressing the political aspects of the film's story.[5]

Schmitz suffered from episodes of depression in the years leading up to the First World War; in 1915 he was a war correspondent on the Western Front.[6] He died of liver disease on 17 December 1931 in Frankfurt am Main.[7]

———

In German-speaking countries Schmitz remains best known for *Haschisch*, and is almost totally unknown elsewhere. (He did achieve a brief minor notoriety in England for two books he wrote that were critical of the country; one of these, published in 1914, was titled *Das Land ohne Musik: Englische Gesellschaftsprobleme* [*The Land without Music: Problems of English Society*].)

Schmitz was among the first German writers to write in the fantastic style he uses in *Hashish*. As he himself notes in the introduction to this edition, the book was written "between 1897 and 1900 and appeared for the first time in 1902—therefore long before Satanism and the 'Grotesque' genre were fashionable in Germany." In 1904, artist Alfred Kubin married Schmitz's sister, Hedwig, who, owing to a painful chronic illness, later became a morphine addict. For the fourth edition of *Haschisch*, in 1913, Kubin created a new cover and illustrated the stories. This is the edition used for this translation.

The events of *Hashish* begin with a chance encounter. The narrator, who never gives his name, happens to be having a meal in the same restaurant as an older, more sophisticated acquaintance, Count Alta-Carrara. The narrator is an aspiring poet and the count recites some lines from an early poem, lines about pleasures the soul remembers from a previous lifetime. The sentiments in these lines prompt the count to invite the narrator to join him in a night of amusements with friends. The pair go to a large house where they take hashish and listen to stories, some of them related by the count.

These stories are presented in long, sinuous sentences that often resolve themselves with unexpected, near-paradoxical juxtapositions. They are sensational, at times hallucinatory even while relentlessly logical; they are at times sexually graphic, always psychologically astute, and often dazzling in their intellectual intricacy. The narrator and the count are outside some of the stories, lazing on divans in the company of other hashish users; other times they are inside the stories as participants. The stories are not moored in time—they cover a span of roughly a century and a half (and at one point the narrator seems to see himself in the future, giving a speech); some of the characters inside the stories are aware of moving from one century to another and treat the matter quite casually. Names and identities are just as shifting as time. Alta-Carrara in particular has many names. When the narrator questions this, another character responds,

> Why must he always have the same name? Here his name is Count of Saint-Germain. You must have met him in the nineteenth century. There he calls himself Alta-Carrara. The other day a lady from the fourteenth century was here who called him Buonaccorso Pitti. You see, everything is relative. . . .

While the narrator does participate in some of the action, his presence is rarely crucial. Most often he is an observer, an onlooker. Recurring references to peep shows, peepholes, and the like serve to remind us that the protagonist is in reality almost immobile (in the framing narrative, outside the stories proper, he moves from divan to gallery seat, back to divan—or all of his movements may be hallucinations; he is never sure), and is for the most part being shown—through words and visions—lessons taken from the extreme actions and experiences of others.

Hashish, like *The One Thousand and One Nights*, is a collection of individual tales. Schmitz unrolls his episodic plots carefully, effectively, and every element included contributes to the overall effect. Yet while the events of each story do resolve and the stories do end, they do not "close," in the current sense of "closure." There is none of the satisfying, cover-closing snap of the kind that would let readers leave the stories behind. Rather, questions linger on; phrases and ideas subtly reappear from one story to the next. Even transitions from related tale to framing story are not always clear.

What is clear, despite these shifts in century and location, names and identities, and word-drunk flights of language—particularly, though not exclusively, in the wild verbal flights of a friar secretly devoted to Satan—that can at times leave the reader struggling for comprehension, is that the narratives here comprise a whole, sketch an arc. At the conclusion of the last story, "The Message," when the narrator—after riding in a cab, "on and on, relentlessly, days, weeks, years"—sits and ponders the encounter he has had with a strange messenger, the events he thinks back over are not just those of one night, or even of one century. Rather they are—however fragmentary—all the events of the narratives that preceded his panicked flight. When he resolves to better his life after these tales and encounters, after receiving the (so the messenger tells him) inexplicably delayed message, the narrative that concludes the volume suggests a fitting, if surrealistically proffered, alternative.

———

In the end, again like *The One Thousand and One Nights*, the most important action is that unfolding in snippets in the framing story between the tales themselves. Whereas between Scheherazade's tales readers are reminded that she is telling her tales in order to stave off her husband's intention to kill her, in *Hashish*, we see the narrator's self-examination, his questioning of the life he is living, and his struggle to lift himself into a higher kind of existence.

His journey from station to station of experience, as it were, his acquisition of "bittersweet wisdom" as he at one point refers to the morals and lessons of these powerful stories, begins with drugs, moves into an illustration of the idea that imagination is greater than reality; through the perils and paradoxes, the power and contradictions of sex and religion—most often together rather than separately; to an awareness of death and the costs of living; to the loss of dreams (or their abandonment for the sake of some better reality) and the dilution of the good things of the world and their replacement by poor substitutes. This last in a story that includes a surrealistic scene of ideas incarnated, where the narrator finds himself in a hidden mountain eyrie where ideas, revolutions, dreams, and fantasies are literally bottled and sold. In the end, he is left with the written word (and, he doesn't let us forget, sex and money) to make his way through the world. At the end of the book, instead of a great revelation about the plots of the stories, we are shown a simple truth about the narrative voice: it is that of a born teller of tales.

NOTES

1. Quoted in "Bürgerliche Welt und Bohème," by Uwe Pralle, http://www .deutschlandfunk.de/buergerliche-welt-und-boheme.700.de.html?dram :article_id=82939. Unless otherwise credited, all translations from sources are my own.

2. Excerpts from Schmitz's journals from http://gutenberg.spiegel.de/ buch/tagebucher-1896-1906-auszuge-6761/1.

3. http://www.faz.net/aktuell/feuilleton/geisteswissenschaften/oskar-a-h-schmitz-und-karl-abraham-daemonen-in-der-psychoanalyse-1492994.html.

4. Wolfgang Martynkewicz, "Die dunklen Seiten eines Dandys: Der Schriftsteller Oscar A. H. Schmitz in der Analyse bei Karl Abraham," *Jahrbuch der Psychoanalyse*, Bd. 55 (Stuttgart, 2007), 113–142.

5. Schmitz, "*Potemkin* and Tendentious Art" (trans. Alex H. Bush), in *The Promise of German Cinema: German Film Theory 1907–1933*, ed. Anton Kaes, Nicholas Baer, and Michael Cowan (Oakland: University of California Press, 2016), 355–356; Walter Benjamin, "Reply to Oscar A. H. Schmitz," trans. Rodney Livingstone, ibid., 356–358.

6. http://www.weilburg-lahn.info/pdf/biografie_schmitz.pdf.

7. Some sources place his death on the 18th.

HASHISH

Oh! là là! que d'amours splendides j'ai rêvées!

Arthur Rimbaud

PREFACE TO THE FOURTH EDITION

Today I neither would nor could write this book, which was created between 1897 and 1900 and appeared for the first time in 1902—therefore long before Satanism and the "grotesque" genre were fashionable in Germany. This is perhaps because my imagination now blooms in less exuberant abundance, perhaps because a more universal worldview somewhat inhibits the purely aesthetic fluttering from excitement to excitement. Nevertheless, I am pleased that I wrote this book as a twenty-four-year-old. I am now set the necessary task of bringing its reappearance into harmony with my more recent, occasionally expressed, and vigorously attacked views on the boundaries between art, morality, and religion. A work of art can in itself, as is today being preached *ad nauseam*, neither be immoral nor irreligious. In fact, as a work of art it has nothing at all to do with morality and religion. It is, however, possible that an immoral use can perhaps be made of it, and limited minds, because of their beliefs, may take offense at this. In this book I certainly do not undertake to shake the foundations of family and marriage, when I as an artist look to extract my material from among the curiosities that lie outside the family. Just as little do I express contempt for religion—which would completely contradict my own religious views—when I show a blasphemous crowd of wicked young people at the moment where they think to commit the sin against the Holy Spirit sinking adoringly to their knees before the omnipotence of God. A monsignor in Rome once assured me that my depiction, as it also correctly portrays the Devil in detail, is contrary to nothing in Catholic dogma. A believer will even be edified that God hardly allows the greatest of all sins, that against the Holy Spirit. At any rate, this book was written only for educated adults. Its outward appearance will keep it out of the nursery, its price should make it inaccessible to adolescents, and its style will hardly awaken the interest of the semi-educated. Thereby enough has been done to meet the legitimate demands of social morality.

I address myself now to experienced men. If this little book seems worthy of such an honor and if the fate of his beloved is, while still having to live in this world of Christian morality, to bloom in wild grace beyond the bounds of social morality, he could place it on her dressing table. To give it to young sisters and daughters who should order their fates within these bounds would be reprehensible. To make a gift of it to his wife is largely unnecessary, often risky, but that of course always depends on the wife.

And to you, lovely idler who has by chance come upon this preface and has now been enticed into reading further, I say this: If you cannot help yourself, then read this secretly, the way you sometimes sneak into a not entirely aboveboard ball where you do not belong. As long as you yourself know that this is only an escapade for you, that you don't intend to brag about it and so become a bad example for other women, then why the devil shouldn't you read it? But if you are more inclined to take the point of view of hypocritical licentiousness and your every third expression is "that's nothing!" or if you are one of those chattering geese who repeatedly emphasize that a woman is above all else human and so has the same moral nature as a man, then we have nothing to say to one another.

After the performance of a play of mine which addresses the "Don Juan" problem, a modern mother came up to me and told me how delighted her eighteen-year-old daughter had been by the performance and with what excitement the questions I raised were discussed at the dinner table. I was quite shocked, particularly as the child herself approached me, and I earnestly cautioned the good lady not to give my works to young girls. "Oh, we are quite liberal," she replied. "But I am not," I said in sheepish embarrassment. "Please don't allow your daughter to talk to me about my play. I know of no subject I could not address with a woman, but I don't feel qualified to help with anyone's sexual education."

Why are these simple questions so confused today? In a healthy functioning society there are also a number of lawmakers and moral philosophers who are against unexpected things. It is precisely their colorful preposterousness that provokes artists in particular. To ban them is hypocritical, philistine, and, moreover, futile. By no means should one shout about them. So it is also necessary to require of the artist that the form he uses to address such material, and of the publisher that the manner in which he brings it to the market, should respect its distance from the prevailing morality. A man at the family dinner table does not discuss how he dined with an "interesting" lady the day before. In the same way we must prevent books that deal with highly sensitive subjects from falling into the wrong hands. The English system is quite wrong, because it murders art. There the artist is simply prohibited the representation of such things, and young girls are permitted to read and to view everything. This instead of allowing the artist freedom of representation but sometimes forbidding young girls access. French society became so free and witty because young girls were strictly excluded. English society is so boring and monotonous because "spinsters" have to be involved in everything.

The author who sets out on daring paths must cultivate a particularly refined style, and with that he has fulfilled the obligations of morality and tact. Anything more is the concern of publishers, booksellers, parents, and guardians. So, for you laughing courtesans, I lay this little book from my youth open on your breast. For you, self-reliant and clever ladies, perhaps I will secretly slip it under your pillows!

Frankfurt am Main
January 1913
O.A.H.S.

THE HASHISH CLUB

One evening in the winter of 189* I found myself in an out-of-the-way Paris eatery. As I, giving no notice to my surroundings, occupied myself with my meal to the exclusion of everything else, I heard near me a quiet voice addressing the waiter. Despite the foreign accent, the adroit, elegant mode of expression, one that betrayed an intimacy with the boulevards, caught my attention and I recognized the slim, discreet blond dandy, already somewhat aged, as Count Vittorio Alta-Carrara. I observed him without being seen as he assembled his courses. The emphatic verticals of his lines had intensified since our last meeting, and his unsurpassed sense of style did justice to his disposition. His thin long legs tapered into a pair of very narrow boots, while his almost fleshless fingers ended in pointed, arch-shaped nails. His thin lips, which displayed no sensuousness, had, in addition to their "ennui," a certain degree of bitterness that allowed his cool personality to appear almost humane, somewhat approachable.

"Ah, so you are in Paris," the count said, and expressed astonishment simply out of graciousness, although between our last meeting and this evening in Paris stretched several years and countries.

We had first come to know one another in a Roman salon where, in accordance with the custom of the country, we had stood for an hour, each with a teacup in hand, side by side amidst rare statuary. I later learned that he had a Calabrian father who had begotten him during a period of mysterious enthusiasm for the big, blonde-haired women of the north with a rather inferior Norwegian who was blonde and slim enough to allow the fanciful southerner the scent of the Apples of Freyja, at least from afar.—

Another time I saw the count in a remote Dutch museum, where he was seeking the remaining scraps of an obscure engraver, Allaert van Assen. This master—so he assured me—had depicted a Hell filled with ingenious tortures that evidently proved pain was a great pleasure, so much so that only foolish people could not crave the pleasures of eternal damnation. When this Satanist strayed into Spain, the Inquisition, with snow-cold poultices on hearts and minds, very prudently and slowly burned him and destroyed or defaced his works. The last time I had seen the count had been in a manuscript archive in a small German town, where he had unearthed an Arabic codex which, so he swore, made all European erotic literature superfluous.

This evening Alta-Carrara was not very talkative. All his attention seemed concentrated on his food which, prepared to his particular specifications, seemed to satisfy him completely. He suddenly broke off eating his chestnut soup, which appeared to have awakened some memory in him: "Did you not once compose a verse— something like . . .

> . . . *and a pleasure, gathered in a thousand spring times,*
> *That the soul recalls from a previous existence,*
> *Transfigures with yellow morning light*
> *The deeps that blackly surround life* . . . ?

"You see, a hashish paradise that presents this pleasure of a thousand spring times, that would be great art. But we all only talk about it, we do not create it. The new art must depose hashish, opium . . . !"

I was surprised. I had never heard this pale man speak so forcefully, with such unmistakable sincerity. And this happened because of a verse that had left him unsatisfied. Until now I had been inclined to regard him as being just an educated aesthetic dandy. But now it almost seemed to me that I heard from him a cry for infinity, out of that singular pain that today bewilders so many spirits, a pain that previously had found compensation in certain more refined branches of Christianity, and perhaps would still find it today had not certain chapels been (who knows for how long) closed.—I had not had the opportunity to meet Alta-Carrara's eyes this evening, and only now observed that almost exhausted stare that struggles to contact horizons beyond the human, the transition to which only the satanic drugs that the count had already mentioned would permit.—We had finished our meals almost simultaneously, while Alta-Carrara had again assumed the deliberate restraint of a solitary man who believes himself to have been very polite because he has spoken a few words.

"I am going to spend the evening with friends," he suddenly said. "Perhaps you have the interest and the time to take part in our society."

Again I was surprised. Alta-Carrara hardly knew me. He could judge no more of me with any certainty than the quality of my tailor. This ever-deliberate man was not capable of rash politeness. So I had to presume a relationship between that verse, which he perhaps took as indicative of my personality, and the character of the society into which he wanted to introduce me.

We went to the Batignolles quarter. Along the way I had hoped to hear a few preparatory remarks about Alta-Carrara's circle of friends. He spoke, however, with superficial, almost elegant lightness about a variety of things, yet without saying anything foolish. I felt he did this only to avoid another silence.—After we had climbed the six flights of stairs of a modern apartment house we were shown into a long, studio-style space. In the dim light of the red-filtered candles I saw several men in what looked to me to be comfortable oriental dress resting on low cushions. Between the couches were stools with hookahs and steaming bowls of incense. A mild smell of burning resin mingled with the lighter smoke of English cigarettes. On the dark red walls hung deep-black etchings and engravings, in which barely discernible images, like the visions of an incubus, stared down on us. In the corners, between exotic plants, I could make out antique musical instruments like strange reptiles. There was barely a stir as we entered. Casual greetings were exchanged. Alta-Carrara gestured silently as he introduced me. Then we lowered ourselves down onto pillows. From a table standing between us the count took some tablets of hashish and, smiling, offered me the bowl.

"These recumbent wanderers," he said in an undertone, "are in a state of animated awareness that cannot be termed intoxication. They have swallowed only very small doses of hashish. You can hear that they speak in logical, sequential sentences, though they frequently find more and stranger connections than they would otherwise recognize. If we are lucky, we will find ourselves in something like an assembly of suddenly enlightened artists with fabulous words flowing from their lips, the splendor of which they themselves will tomorrow barely be able to imagine. Others forgo the pleasures of hashish and marvel at the effect it produces in the rest. Those who are capable of doing so will try, through music or strange tales, to lead the visions of the others in particular directions. Take a look through this door into the next room; there you will find those who want to sink entirely into the abyss of the unconscious."

In the twilight I saw sleeping people stretched out in front of Venetian mirrors.

"The colorful glass flowers on the mirrors make them believe they are submerged in fabulous ponds," said the count. "The two men quietly circulating are helpful servants who protect them against heat and thirst, because in their paralysis of will they would prefer to let their lips burn than to lift the drink before them to their mouths."

I decided, like my neighbors, to heighten my senses with only a small dose of hashish, to clear away the inhibited conceptions of the often unbidden practical intellect; in short, to enjoy a heightened existence.

There was great calm in the room. Occasionally individual French words were uttered, the pronunciation of which told me that some of those present were foreign. I dreamily passed what may have been half an hour, while in the corner of the room a clavichord and a viola da gamba played an old-fashioned Italian divertimento. I felt with particular pleasure how this music penetrated, perfused, glowed within me and the objects surrounding me. The way everything now glowed seemed quite natural to me. This was the true color of life. Previously, everything had slumbered. Everything around me was airy and, above all, quite benevolent. The opacity of objects appeared to have been abrogated; everything was colored glass, nothing was concealed behind anything; the phrases I heard were precise and simple, like mathematical theorems, and seemed resolvable into numbers. At a glance I clearly saw relationships that otherwise are the product of laborious deliberation. Words sparkled in the various colors of all languages. The syllable "*kirche*" sounded as large and as bright as "*église*," as mistrustfully puritanical as "church." The letters "word" simultaneously contained the talisman-like "*logos*," the rune-like "*waurd*," the sharp flying "*mot*," the somewhat plump, frilly "*parole*." Every syllable resounded with the undertones of half rhymes. I smelled, saw, tasted every word, felt it as silk or as marble. I no longer saw only surfaces, but rather whole bodies, from all sides simultaneously. And this sudden richness of reality, from which I in no way stepped out, made me exuberantly happy and grateful, so much so that I would have gladly done good for others, providing I could have remained stretched out on the divan. Incidentally, I was fully aware of where I was. It seemed to me that I wore a pair of colored glasses. If I wished I could, however, also have peered over the lenses and seen how indefinite, confused, and fusty life really is. I was the master of my will and could according to my mood look at things as they truly were or as colored.

The dark red wallpaper glowed, as if the walls were made of glass behind which fabulous suns sank in great bursts of embers. Against this background a great head suddenly rose, one so enormously enlarged that it filled my entire field of vision. Within that rich, reddish beard I observed firm, thin lips. The pale face was nearly rigid, and in my memory of it, it at times took on a cadaverous sheen of green or violet. This man said that he had been born in Germany, so could I please forgive him his imperfect pronunciation of French. His clearly understandable words aroused my curiosity. I deliberately once again clung firmly to reality and chose to listen carefully to the man, whom I recognized as the same one who had earlier played the clavichord. As easy as it was for me to follow his words in my mind, I was glad that I did not have to move my body. He told me a story from which scenes and conversations have remained in my memory with great clarity, in a way that it so seldom retains my own experiences. I have succeeded in recovering these details:

THE DEVIL'S LOVER

Fifteen years ago hardship drove me to accept a position as musical director in a provincial British town. The relatively small-scale maliciousness of the population of my native town had permitted me to combine a fairly unconstrained way of life with visits to polite drawing rooms. Yes, I allowed myself to bring into them a slight whiff of the outside and to claim certain privileges of a spoiled, naughty child. This is all now a half-generation in the past. From this setting, I found myself suddenly dropped down in the most bourgeois English atmosphere, the character of which was the very definition of the word "respectability." Imagine a town where houses are coated in a sooty reddish-black and illuminated through tiny windows of a stunted Gothic style. Opening them means pushing up the panes, so that putting one's head through is to a certain extent to place it under a guillotine. Imagine streets of an unhealthy, as it were disinfected, cleanliness recalling the sick blandness of certain skins that never sweat, their pores tightly closed against perspiration. Through these streets moves a silent population. Everyone is properly dressed, to an embarrassing degree. The men wear suits the color of dirt or of rain-soaked roads. Their faces must have once frozen in a moment of desperate spiritual apathy, appalled by some terrible incident. You could believe you are everywhere seeing fossils. No coffee houses or cafés enliven the streets, only reeking whiskey bars. My days played out in a boarding house. Around its table gathered a company of poor, blond, lymphatic men. The red pustules in their watery, beardless faces, their long limbs, and in particular their flat, emotionless voices that could have been those of machines at first prompted only a cold stare from me. Almost all day long, silent servants carried covered bowls and platters with gigantic bloody roasts through the gloom of the seemingly endless corridors and dining rooms. Even at nine o'clock in the morning thick stews and heavy pastries were consumed, so that from very early on I was in that dulled state that comes over one after too rich a meal. A bitter black beer, thick as porridge, lured the mind disposed to straightforward thinking into a swamp. The blood thickened into stagnation; one felt the brain as a warm heavy mass in the head, in which a spiky evil thing is stuck fast: spleen.

My employment consisted of managing a musical club founded on the German pattern, in which the society of H. ostensibly joined together for the cultivation of classical composers. The actual reason was for that mindless flirting so beloved by the provincial English bourgeois because it continually dissipates the instincts, without any demand for further discharges. My stubborn refusal to otherwise participate in any social life, my rather extravagant neckties and vests, soon prompted the circulation of dubious rumors about me. Although all houses were open to me, the interesting stranger in this town that was perishing from curiosity and boredom, I felt mildly attracted to only one circle, one that didn't exist for polite society because only the most despised people belonged to it. In a cellar in the most noxious suburb there gathered the members of a small, hungry company of actors whose often rather grotesque morals always attracted me much more than did the carefully circumscribed ones of any bloodless society. These actors, half-degenerate talents, were devoted to the only panacea that exists against the oppression of English life: whiskey. I passed a number of winter nights with them, usually more sober than they were, in the smoky dim cellar, nights that otherwise might have driven me to suicide, and I never left those haggard boozers before hearing them, their faces distorted and with drunken emphasis, shout out jumbled renditions of their favorite roles. When I, overtaken by fatigue, would emerge into the pure winter night, I could still make out, in distant howling under the hard snow, verses from *Hamlet* and *King Lear*. I often regretted these excesses, which made me sleep away half the next day. But time and again I fled to the actors, because when evening arrived, those wet misty evenings with their showers of cold and terror, that was when the most foolish of ghosts entered my room, the one whose name we are ashamed to admit, and which seems to target the Germanic races in particular: sentimentality. How often had I spent the afternoon with a book that took me far from reality, but when twilight came I silently felt how the damp-cold hands of that ghost appeared to want to caress my forehead, to cover my eyes to prevent me from reading any further. A word would perhaps arouse some weakness of desire, and I would fall under its cruel power for the evening. Or while playing piano the sound of an indifferent voice would come from the courtyard, or I would breathe in the fragrance of tea, or a cigarette, and I would be a slave to a force whose horror is never mentioned, because one is as content to smile before it as over some sweet foolishness. Yet I contend that this insidious fiend pushes us into such intoxication when we try to remain sober, that he awakens in us the fear of being left alone, because we know that he is lying about on the furniture, he brings back fragrances from moments we, thank God, have forgotten, brings foolish melodies winging in, and in the wallpaper dandles forms that call out to us, pityingly, that we are already leading failed lives. We cannot endure this, we run from it; everything that happenstance then throws against us we are entitled to overcome for a few hours. And then, back home, this absurd being insults us—as though we were harming the best of ourselves—and out of protest against this spinsterish sentimentality we sully ourselves as best we can.

Every day I expected that there would be a reversal of my life circumstances, because I could not imagine that these earnest, conservative merchant families would find their musical needs fulfilled for very long by such a dubious being as myself.

One morning an extraordinary event interrupted this winter. I received a letter postmarked as being from the town. The handwriting was obviously disguised. Under the conventional stiff correctness of the English calligraphy I observed a striking flexibility of strokes, fantastically created capital letters that surprised me. I looked in vain for a signature. The letter read:

"Without a doubt, sir, you are the most remarkable person in H., which by the way, isn't saying very much. Since I returned from a trip last week I have noticed that everywhere the imagination of the town concerns itself almost exclusively with you. I have not seen you but I am told you are deathly ugly. I would like to meet you. As the exterior of a person—particularly the non-Anglo-Saxon races—very easily deters me, I would like to talk with you without having to see you. As to how, you let me worry about that. For the present simply write me back and tell me whether it seems worth your while to

meet with someone who will reveal nothing more to you than that she is a lady." "It seems worth it to me," I wrote back, without hesitation, because even a bad joke would change my life in some way. I did not have to search very long for the hole in the tree in James Park where I was to deposit my answer.

"I'm sure you are smart enough," the letter concluded, "not to interrupt the charm of this adventure by stalking the collector. Should you spoil the story through some indiscretion, I will then have to regret a failed diversion."

The next day I received the following invitation: "Monday afternoon at six o'clock a coupé will be waiting at the corner of Pier Road and King Street. The coachman will open the door when you give him the password 'Miramare.'" I indeed found a coupé there on the appointed day in the darkness of the early winter evening under a gaslight. The driver, immobile, staring straight ahead, resembled an Egyptian basalt deity. At my call of "Miramare" I saw him make a quick mechanical movement with his hand. The door opened by itself. The electrically illuminated interior had reseda-colored upholstery that gave off a slight tangy aroma. The door immediately closed behind me and the carriage was set in motion. On a corner tray I found cigarettes. I wanted to pay attention to our route, but when I pushed back the curtains I found that brightly polished wood panels were set into the carriage doors in place of windows. There was no inside handle to open the door. So I was a prisoner until it should occur to the basalt driver to push the button. Only an opaque ventilation apparatus set into the roof connected me with the outside world. The almost silent motion of the rubber wheels made it impossible to distinguish whether we were traveling over pavement or whether we had left the town behind. The trip was considerably longer than any simple route through the town, but the driver could well have been instructed to proceed via detours in order to lead my suspicions astray. My stay in the fragrant luminosity of this rolling boudoir, however, was quite tolerable. I tried a cigarette, the quality of which I found to be excellent. The carriage suddenly came to a stop. I heard voices outside and the electric lamp went out. The door opened. I saw a snowy wood, a piece of the night sky, and another coupé. After a few moments, gliding like some exotic animal, a black-clad figure approached. It was so thickly shrouded that I could see neither age nor physique. The carriage door immediately closed behind it and the carriage drove on. The being had settled next to me in the darkness. I decided to let it speak first. In the interior nothing could be perceived but the rustle and aroma of heavy silk. Then a confident, rather deep female voice said,

"Give me your matches, please."

I felt her hand on my arm. She secreted my matches, it seemed to me, within her robes.

"Give me your revolver!" she said, sharp and determined.

"Your revolver," she urged.

I assured her that I would never carry a revolver, because I, owing to my excitability, would do myself more harm than good by doing so.

"Except today," she said, half ironically.

"I had expected, as a worst case, this to be a malicious joke," I explained. "This walking stick would have been sufficient to deal with that. I deliver it to you with pleasure."

"Thank you, but I am not afraid of a stick."

"But facing a revolver?"

"Such an instrument," she quickly replied, "so easily gives any adventure the complexion of a *faits divers* for the morning papers."

In this moment I noticed that she laid something hard on the corner tray. I quietly raised my hand to feel the object, and carelessly made some noise by doing so.

"What are you doing?" she asked.

"I am looking for my gloves."

I immediately regretted making this stupid excuse.

"I would like to turn on a light," she cried, laughing, "just to see if you are blushing now." I felt like a schoolboy.

"I confess to having been exposed," I said. "But does it not also reveal a weakness, that you felt it necessary to bring a revolver with you, while I came unarmed?"

"In one respect you can already record a victory," she replied, "in that you now have my trust. I do believe that you are unarmed."

"May I shake your hand?"

"So you can understand me in a flash? Well, I am wearing fur gloves. For you, then, a masked hand whose shape tells you nothing."

I could already see that I was dealing with no Bovary, but rather a woman of great deliberation and wily subtlety. From time to time I fell silent for several minutes. This seemed to make her nervous.

"Perhaps you have had a bad day today?" she asked.

"On the contrary, the best I've had since moving to H. And you?"

"I'm a little bored."

"For your amusement, then, I will tell you that at this moment you are feeling exactly what men so often feel when facing women. Out of fear of being seen as banal they are afraid to speak the necessary first words. I know women are very amused by this fear in men, because they realize this means they are being taken seriously. So they would not consider whether the conversation was banal even if the subject was the weather. I will now also be a little critical, the way a woman is. Ask me simply how I like H., whether it is as beautiful in Germany . . ."

"But you can also say all that without being asked," she replied, baffled and a little insulted.

"It doesn't seem at all important to me to talk," I said, laughing. "It does not bore me in the slightest to silently roll through unknown regions with one unknown to me, about whom I can imagine at will that she is Semiramis or La Belle Otero, and leave it to her to supply me with the most extraordinary surprises. But if you wish to talk, I am at your disposal."

"Is that actually rudeness?" she asked, naïvely.

"As I do not yet know you, I find it more interesting to think about Cleopatra than about a governess in the novels of Mrs. Bradford."

"I will now freely offer you a hand," she suddenly said. "For my part, I believe this adventure holds promise."

Cool, dry fingers slid slowly over mine. I felt one of those slender, almost too bony hands with their long fingers, slightly convex at the joints, whose tremulous agility seems to constantly produce different shapes.

"Do you believe that I'm beautiful?" she asked, while in the darkness I played with her hand, which slowly warmed itself in mine.

"No," I replied, "but your hand reveals a soul that makes beauty superfluous."

"Well," she cried, and seemed simultaneously indignant and embarrassed. She moved away. As I leaned equally far back into my corner she began again, nervously: "Why do you think I have initiated this whole business?"

"Presumably out of curiosity?"

"Presumably? Do you take me, then, to be so indolent?"

Rather than answering her, I wrapped my arms tightly about her. While she resisted, I worked my way to her veiled face and pressed my lips to hers. Her resistance grew weaker under the force of the kiss, during which I inhaled the powdery smell of cheeks gone past the bloom of youth. There was something so naïvely eager in her small fine mouth that I had the—perhaps erroneous—impression that she was discovering the delights of a kiss for the first time. She suddenly pushed me away, as if I had somehow injured her.

"I no longer like you," she said curtly.

"Because you cannot satisfy your curiosity as quickly as you had believed?"

"And you? Are you satisfied?"

"Nowhere near!" I replied, coolly.

"And you say that so calmly."

"Quite, because I am certain of satisfaction."

"That's a bit much."

"You think so?"

I again took her into my arms. She tried to break loose.

"Let me go or I will ring the coachman."

"So ring."

Without any movement by her that I could perceive, the carriage came to a stop. In the same moment the door opened to allow her to get out, then closed. The electric lamp glowed, and the carriage quickly set off again. I found myself again a solitary prisoner in the fragrant brightness of a boudoir. Had I, through too rapid action, spoiled the adventure, during which I perhaps had embraced the idol of my dreams, or had an ancient courtesan swooped down on me? For the most part, however, I tended to imagine a green-eyed deviant with tiny cat's teeth. My thoughts were suddenly interrupted by the carriage coming to a stop. The door opened, I stepped out, and found myself on a familiar street corner. Before I had time to give the coachman a coin, the carriage departed. I stood on the street like a beggar who, awakened from a fairy-tale dream, no longer knows how to again make his way in the real world.

I must have been brooding over the adventure for a week when, one morning, I received another letter from the unknown one. In an area far from the previous quarter the coupé would be waiting at the same hour.

I was again made prisoner in the bright rolling boudoir for half an hour. When the carriage came to a stop I expected a recurrence of the events of the previous encounter. Instead, I found myself in the courtyard of a palatial building. Before me rose a staircase which was illuminated by two candelabras. It led up to a mezzanine level. There two servants waited for me, and they silently opened a glass door. I stepped through it and came to a bright, very warm stairway. I was propelled, as it were, through a double door into a dark room. My feet felt thick carpeting. I inhaled that singular aroma of fine wood and heavy silk that prevails in lavish, rarely occupied rooms. I slowly felt my way to a chair. Then I heard a sound as if a door in the far wall was pushed open and then closed.

"Where are you, my friend?" asked the deep voice I knew, in a tone of familiarity that surprised me after our last parting.

"Stay where you are; I'll find you."

I could hear her as she crossed the carpet, then I felt her hands in my hair.

"Follow me!" she whispered.

And I again clasped that thin hand that led me on. I breathed in the warm intimate atmosphere that emanates from women who have remained whole winter days in their perfumed chambers wearing light robes. We stepped into an adjoining room, one so very hot that it must have housed damp tropical plants. She drew me down on a divan. The dark was so impenetrable that I could not even guess where the windows might be.

"I have now seen you," she began. "Someone showed you to me."

"That is a compliment," I replied.

"How so?"

"In that you nevertheless chose to continue the adventure."

"I truly do find you as ugly as death. But this is your chance with me."

"Then you are depraved."

"And the depravity of loving you is called Satanism," she said, laughing softly.

"I fear that for you depravity is only literary," I replied, suddenly skeptical.

"I don't understand."

"Perhaps you have been living in literary circles, in London or in Paris, where it was until recently considered very elegant to indulge in unusual sorts of depravity."

"Never. Only financiers or at best naval officers have come near me. A part of my life has been lived in America. I have never been to Paris, neither would I care to go; I imagine it to be a silly place. I have only passed through London. My fortune has permitted me a few eccentricities, but I have not known until this moment what literary depravity is."

"All the better," I replied. "But how do you know of Satanism? Is that word still heard in the vocabulary of American salons?"

"I am going to enjoy telling you this," she began, pleasantly. "Even as a child the fantasies of Catholicism appealed to me. But believe me, it is nothing but a pastime for me—essentially I wouldn't give two cents for it—I am a Protestant, and one out of conviction. Later on, I randomly bought Catholic writings with highly promising, virtually indecent titles, which then of course for the most part disappointed me. This tempted me even more. It annoyed me that these authors seemed to be keeping to themselves the secrets that they claimed to know and about which Protestantism says nothing. It's probably just all talk, I often told myself. But I absolutely wanted to see through the tricks of these people. So I came across a book on demonology by Pater Sinistrari d'Ameno . . ."

"You know him?" I interrupted, surprised.

"There I found the description of secret meetings of women with very strong-minded beings called incubi. Never had I heard anything that inflamed my imagination more. To have a supernatural association somewhere apart from society, one which can be gauged by no human measure, that therefore also violates no human moral laws and can't compromise a lady socially—because what a Catholic writer speaks of as being a mortal sin doesn't hold for us Protestants—that seemed to me such an incredibly ingenious idea, worthy of a truly perfect God: a way to reward particularly intelligent believers who love to conceal their actions from the general public. From that moment on my life's only purpose was to sample this unearthly joy. For years I listened to everything unusual that made its way into my circle, until some time ago when a palmist foretold that the most extraordinary event in my life would occur this year. I set out on a journey in order to meet the miraculous. I recently returned, exhausted and disappointed."

"What you must have got up to on this journey!" I interjected, amused.

"Don't interrupt me." She went on, excitedly: "When I came here to H., I heard about you. I was frightened; your name haunted me when I was alone. I was convinced that you must be associated with the longed-for event. In any case, I knew we should speak. Perhaps you were meant to be my tool; perhaps Pater Sinistrari spoke only symbolically. One could certainly enter into an almost supernatural relationship with a living being in order to escape the disappointments and dangers of the sensible world, simply by closing one's eyes. Don't you think so?"

I did not at all feel like someone who had come to a romantic liaison. This blend of cold, calculating depravity with caustic speculation and Protestant bourgeois narrowness, this uncomfortable feeling of having been summoned to serve as, as it were, a tool, could really upset one's equilibrium. To avoid an embarrassing silence, I said, "You have unfortunately robbed yourself of the possibility of gratifying your imagination—by seeking to have a look at me."

"How could I allow you into my house," she said, sounding very surprised, "without knowing that you are a gentleman?"

I could hardly keep from laughing. This Anglo-Saxon bore the prejudices of her class through all four dimensions.

"And now you are convinced of that?"

"Not only of that," she whispered, suddenly energized again. I felt how close she was to me in the dark. "I now also know that you truly are the chosen one for my experience. I have put out the lights so that you can imagine you are embracing your ideal—not a woman about whom a thousand things would disturb you. And those primal embraces which no reality can exhaust, I want to steal them for myself—such a theft! I have indeed seen you, seen you as you are, and I thought, 'Satan!'"

She was breathless. I impetuously threw my arms around her and was suddenly filled with the nameless desire to throw myself into the gaping abyss before me with my eyes closed.

"Hush . . . not another word . . .," I groaned, as if in dark fear of waking—"don't spoil this." And I pressed my lips against hers. Unresisting, silent, she belonged to me. I felt I was in an impenetrable night, within which I could imagine fantastic, dreamlike landscapes. For the first time, I held the ideal woman in my arms, this dark, great, remote eternal one, which no other single woman could ever fully embody. Everything that at other times had poured impotent dreams and disappointing realities into me now burned with joy. I have never lavished myself so mindlessly in a feeling of dissolution as with this lean, supple, unfamiliar body which, for me, contained no personality, which truly was the ideal. I cried aloud, unfamiliar barbaric words similar, so she later claimed, to the natural sounds that she had heard from savages in the mindless delirium of their sacred dances, an involuntary sound arising from the highest excitations of the soul, those that touch on the greatest mysteries. She had forgotten these sounds. However, they would come back to her, she said, when she experienced the taste of certain poisons on her tongue, just as some memories are associated with melodies or scents. I myself can only compare my feelings with those I once had as I was hanging by my fingertips over an abyss in the Alps and in the face of death saw my entire life, running backward, flash by in an instant. Thus all the women I had known passed by me in this embrace, and I felt I was possessing them all. Embraces I'd experienced repeated themselves in more perfect unions; failed adventures shaped themselves anew; queens once desired but unapproachable fell into my arms; at the end came wondrous, veiled, dreamlike women. These were the lovers of my boyhood dreams, whom I earlier and more fervently embraced than any of the living ones. Only he who knows such fantastic cravings as a child can measure the gratifications of these hours against the power of these former desires, which transcend the desires of any actual love.

I do not know how or in which moments I fell asleep in the arms of this woman. I awoke suddenly; I

presently had a sense of exalted hot fragrances. Now I heard a murmur of garments, the movement of a door. Countless glowing lamps surrounded me. I was shocked to suddenly find myself in a cramped, garishly lit room where hideous masks grinned at me from all sides. Their brown, hairy faces protruded from between colossal hunting bows, multicolored plumes of feathers and other fantastic implements of savage tribes. This was the boudoir of my woman friend. I walked back into the room next door and found myself in a bright, somewhat peculiar Louis xv salon the color of strawberries. A servant entered and said, "Madame sends her regrets. She is unable to receive you today."

I followed him into the courtyard, where the coupé awaited me. The coachman drove me back to the same street corner.

Every four to five days I received similar summons to various quarters, but the coupé always took me to the same destination. We talked together less and less. What could two people say who only made use of one another's bodies as a pretext for orgies of the imagination? It was not I, but Satan that this woman loved. And when she lay silent and suffered in the dark before me, when I searched over her lines with my hand, when I felt as though I had found a fallen statue in the grass that grew animated under my touch, then I loved Lais, then cities went up in flames around me, cities where torches were thrown at a sign from this woman, just as flames burned in my soul, and nothing was further from my mind than the desire to possess this woman herself.

Above all, for the first time in my life, she succeeded in satisfying my tormented imagination. The love ecstasies of history and the poetry that always seemed more shocking, more mysterious than mine, I no longer needed to envy like one feeble and born too late; I knew how to make them live again. "Just wait until tonight," I would tell myself when my fantasy squandered itself in idle images, and there were nights when I heard the Adriatic beating against the marble palaces, when I felt thick velvet next to her skin, resplendent velvet beneath which her limbs appeared to swell. A wickedly beautiful dogaressa played with me and was delighted that for her I scorned death, because that could be the cost of her love.—Or the way the scent of Franconian forests rose from her hair; her lines were as soft as the songs German girls once sang at the well in the evening . . . Girls whose love for Our Lady had to be wheedled out of them, girls who can suddenly forget everything, even the secret chapel of their childish prayers and yet are happy to know that the Madonna is still there, smiling—even then they only tardily return to Her when *he* is gone to some foreign land, loving more dazzling women.—And there were fickle hours, when my beloved's sharp, short laugh called forth an impudent duchess of the Régence; a powder with an almost herbal scent gave her skin a morbid smoothness. And I felt as if the room around us was light and snug, a nut in which we swam in some sea, not quite real and certainly very mild. And our embrace was as if permeated with golden threads and encompassed by small flourishes that had the form of almonds. And on such days my beloved was very ticklish.

These experiences would not have been possible had she not possessed a quality that normally cannot easily be forgiven in a woman. The fact was, she herself was in no way perceptible; there was no temper, no joking, no ideas, no wishes, nothing unexpected. Anything she needed she seemed to find without my assistance. Still, something annoyed me: if I regarded her as my tool, even more so was I hers. She beckoned; I came. If she was tired of me, she dismissed me. When I once, on a whim, failed to appear, she wasted not one word on it. After a few days a new invitation would always come. This indifference annoyed me. I decided to provoke her, to make her angry by inventing absurd reasons for stay- ing away. But then, when her hair smelled as if it would glow red in the sun, when her gaunt form clenched me in such nervous haste that I did not know whether she felt the highest of torments or of pleasures, whether she loved me or wanted to punish me, then I forgot all anger, all intention. Then I felt as if I were the confessor who enters the cell of a young witch who must burn the next morning and today wants to gorge herself one more time on passion, something she can still seize on to quickly absorb as much external power as she can, is eager to destroy as much as she possibly can.—My conceit of superiority died away when I found her lethargic and immobile, like a bayadère who has one hot morning rolled in the shade of bizarre plants and, unthinking, devoured too many sweet fruits. She smelled of Indian flowers, she performed curious belly motions, so that she seemed to me to be almost too voluptuous. So I gladly forgot that I perhaps at best held a trifling lady. She did not even exist. At times the thought occurred to me to coach her in the use of certain arousing words in foreign or dead languages. But I realized in time that if I did so the liveliness of my ideal would become literature, theater, a little banter that any prostitute could have learned.—Of course, I had created a particular idea of her for myself, but I really cannot say whether I thought her more beautiful or more ugly than the women I encountered that I sometimes suspected of being her. The extraordinary nature of my pleasures was not at all to be measured against any real standard.

So, although we remained remote from all contact with daily routine where lay the germs that are fatal to human relationships, this most extraordinary of all love stories came to as dull and trivial an end as any sergeant's love affair. The lady became jealous—of my ideal. One day she asked me, like some small-minded seamstress, if I loved her. And with that the story truly came to an end. She had figured out that my pleasures were more glowing and varied than hers. Because of her early curiosity, her senses were now bound to my countenance once and for all. She was tired of always kissing the same being, even if she had called it "Satan" on the honeymoon. I was malicious enough to note that without her "ladylike" caution and curiosity she, like me, could have a harem at her disposal, that then she could today embrace a gentle George Brummell, tomorrow a Roman gladiator. These words drove her into a helpless rage.

"You should now also get to know me, as well," she suddenly said. "And we will see if you still prefer your ideal."

I guessed that she was about to turn on the light.

"Please don't," I cried. "I will run out."

"You don't want to see me?"

"You cannot possibly be as beautiful as I want to believe you are."

"This is outrageous!"

"Yet you were willing to accept the praise due an ideal."

At this point she no doubt feared disappointing me. She left me without saying a word.

I received no further invitations. Weeks passed, and I felt a great void in my life, an ongoing, uninterrupted desolation. I was as sad as if a good lover of mine had died, yet as soon as I thought of this woman all desire left me. I felt something like quiet scorn, a kind of disdain for her all-too-great inferiority, and thinking about her was hardly worth the trouble.

One evening I was alone in the sole restaurant in the town where one could dine after the theater. At a table behind me sat a group of people who had not been there when I had arrived. There were two men in proper evening wear, one with an almost white beard above a clean-shaven jaw, the other a blond young man with a fresh, very English baby-face. Between them sat a pale woman perhaps thirty-five years old. She had dark hair that hung in regular curls straight across her forehead, a thin Celtic face with still, almost staring, brown eyes. She had an extraordinary air of distinction. The almost too long, narrow mouth was decorated with very white, notably small teeth—a face of which one might think it had once been beautiful, because something is lacking and one ascribes that to the passing of years. Most likely, however, it had always been lacking. Her hands were large, yet slim and adorned with a number of opals. These three people had a natural, unpretentious gentility with nothing forced about it, like the neighbors one gladly has at the theater or at the *table d'hôte*, who do not even arouse one's interest. Nevertheless, I felt a compulsion to turn to them. I thought I noticed the lady watching me as well. "Perhaps this is the unknown one," I thought, unconcerned, but this idea naturally came to me in regard to a great number of women. I ordered coffee and took the opportunity, as the waiter cleared the table, to shift position, so that I had the strangers in sight. I noticed that the lady became restless and spoke with sudden urgency to the old gentleman. He paid the bill; the trio left the restaurant.

The following day I received two letters. "The play is finished," read the one in the familiar hand. "I sense I have been recognized; let us drop the masks." The other bore similar, if more natural, apparently unfeigned touches. It contained a formal invitation to a ball from a lady completely unknown to me. This woman appeared to be willing to build an inevitable flirtation, or perhaps even a genuine love affair atop our fantastic orgies. But I preferred not to awaken my fantasy beloved from her grave. Helen had returned to the immaterial. At that moment, I was too spoiled to accept the proffered replacement. I soon left H. I have never seen the lady again.

The narrator fell silent. I had the bleak feeling that something was now irrevocably ended. A life had finished without my dying. The others appeared to be feeling the same thing.

"Another story," someone cried. "This emptiness is just too unbearable!"

We lay as if blind in a dark hole, hungry for the sound of the human voice. Our lives, our wills were numbed. Only imagination—itself barren—was awake and demanded that another, stronger, more sober, should fill it with ideas.

A NIGHT IN THE EIGHTEENTH CENTURY

And someone came and caused a bright carefree music to wash over us, as merry as a gavotte or a passacaglia of the eighteenth century. Around us rose a brilliant church, through which floated well-fed cupids who carried garlands of fruit from box to box. Spiral columns adorned in gold encircled a blue and pink altarpiece. And how amusingly the duchesses knelt before it! How they smelled of powder! And everyone laughed at the splendid priest who entertained them with real conjurer's tricks. I asked the sacristan who was about to pass me for an explanation. As amicably as an urbane Jesuit, he gave me the names of all those in attendance. The priest was the famous Count of Saint-Germain, the splendidly dressed lady the Duchess of Chartres. How had I come here, and what was I doing in a place where I knew no one? (Although I clearly remembered having once seen a copperplate engraving of the count.) Then I remembered that I had just today dined with him, that he had wanted to take me somewhere, to meet his friends. I was annoyed that he had now left me alone.

"Alta-Carrara," I called out irritably.

"Shh, shh," whispered the sacristan soothingly. "Do not give him away. Why must things always have names? Here his name is the Count of Saint-Germain. You must have met him in the nineteenth century. There he calls himself Alta-Carrara. The other day a lady from the fourteenth century was here who called him Buonaccorso Pitti. You see, everything is relative," he said slyly.

"And you, you intolerable windbag," I asked, "to which century do you imagine you belong?"

"I?" he asked haughtily. "The eighteenth, of course. You, sir, on the other hand, are so rude that you are only suited to the nineteenth. Today is—by your leave—15 September 1768."

With a highly affected movement, he left me. I felt an uncontrollable rage toward Alta-Carrara, who was still doing his conjuring act before the altar. I decided to wait for the right moment to take him to task. In the meantime, I removed a long, winding frill from a column, made a noose of it and stood by the church door. It was not long before the count, with a bow, indicated to his audience that the show was at an end. With a self-satisfied smile he walked through the church, followed by the admiring gaze of the duchesses. He was about to step into the street when I threw my noose over his head. He was not sure what was happening to him, but as a man of the world he smiled and spoke with irony, "Your handsome attire tells me you must be from the nineteenth century. How may I be of service to you?"

"Don't act as if you don't know me," I replied angrily. "You promised me . . ."

"Oh, forgive me. These ladies delayed me. Now I'm all yours again. Incidentally, we have plenty of time ahead of us."—He pulled his watch out of his pocket.—"It will be more than twenty years before the revolution. We can amuse ourselves for quite some time yet."

My anger was suddenly replaced by a burning desire for wanton gaiety.

"I want to laugh, cry out, have crimson visions," I declared excitedly. The count was a bit startled.

"We'll see," he soothed.

We climbed into a cabriolet to travel to the Marais. It was night, but the streets were tremendously lively. It had to be a carnival. We were confronted with colorful masked figures who threw flowers into the car. There was exuberant drunken shouting all around us.

"The people know that it will only last another twenty years," said Saint-Germain. "But they imagine it worse than it will actually be. I have, in fact, hoodwinked them into believing that the Jacobins will burn down all of Paris and anyone who tries to flee will be killed."

Saint-Germain could hardly keep himself from laughing at this joke.

"Why did you do that?" I asked, uncomprehending.

"Quite simply to push their merriment into the immoderate. Such small spectacles of world history are the only amusement in my life. Do you think that I want to be as bored as the petit bourgeois Ahasver? The most beautiful thing that I have accomplished is the history of the Albigensians. For I persuaded them that they could cure sin through sin. In the nineteenth century they call that—I believe—homeopathy, *similia similibus*. In fact, those good people imagined that they must violently out-sin all evil. Well, you can imagine the kinds of scenes that were produced. But I won't tire you with descriptions, because today you shall see something similar for yourself."

"We'll see if you can keep your word," I replied, somewhat skeptical.

"You see, I have invited a small, select company to a feast with Count Gilles de Laval, whom you in Germany—so I understand—call Bluebeard. But the guests do not know where they are going, they suspect only that fun lies ahead. Reveal none of this, because my friend Gilles, disguised as a Capuchin monk, would like to remain unrecognized. He doesn't much love the eighteenth century."

Engaged in this conversation we arrived at the Place des Vosges. We drifted along for some time under the arcades without attracting attention, and then took a sedan chair to the Hôtel de Guise in the Marais.

Once we were certain that the bearers were far enough away, we slipped into an alley at the end of which was a very shabby little wooden portal. The count knocked on the door. A hideous old woman opened it. We came into a clammy dark hallway. I followed Saint-Germain through some badly lit, unpleasant passages until he came to a stop, threw off his cloak, and stood there in rich court dress. He smoothed his powdered hair as he considered his face in a hand mirror by the light of a candle, folding and rolling it up again as if it were a silk handkerchief until he found an arrangement that suited him. I was very nervous, impatient. Finally, he opened a door. We stepped into a yellow and silver vestibule. Richly dressed ladies and gentlemen moved before immense candlelight-infused mirrors. A wide staircase led up to a double door that abutted the ceiling. Everyone watched this door expectantly. My desire for merriment was replaced by a fascinated stare before the streams of light that washed over me, before the colorful priceless dresses and the intense aromas of flowers. Spellbound, I let everything flood my senses. Suddenly, an Auvergnat stepped through the door.

"Ah, Castel-Bajac," the call went up.

"Everything is ready," Castel-Bajac said, with the sly look of a cook who has just invented a new delicacy. He opened the double door to the gallery of a great hall. Greatly excited now, all these elegant people climbed the stairs and walked through the door. I mingled with them. We took seats in the gallery and looked down into the empty room. While everything around us up above was decorated in the bright, ostentatious gold-and-mirrors taste of the eighteenth century, and the gay, luxuriant garb corresponded to the same, the hall itself seemed to present a view into a strange, bleak past, into an extravagant, preposterous Gothic scene full of trembling wild creepers and snakes around the pointed arch windows, into the sinister unbridled fantasies of the dying Middle Ages, full of desolate gallows humor. The hall was completely deserted. Countless tall church candles cast a warm yellow light through the space. In the middle stood a long table with a rich bounty and gold dishes that appeared to have been taken from the church. The most striking glass sculptures stood out from between rare, fantastic plants. I was surprised that my illustrious associates weren't taking up places at the table below; they were only watching from the gallery. Suddenly voices could be heard from outside. They seemed to be approaching the hall. Two wide doors drew apart and a crowd of Auvergnat peasants dressed in their Sunday best entered, shy and amazed, led in by Castel-Bajac. They and their wives allowed themselves to be directed to places around the splendid table. They hardly dared speak. From time to time they cast bashful glances at the gallery, from where some excitedly waved down encouragingly. Some great amusement seemed to be expected of them. It was, in fact, very entertaining, the way these stiff people—some serious dignified characters, others crude, uncouth louts—gradually became uninhibited and bolder the more food they consumed. Silent and dignified, servants passed the dishes around, and soon it no longer seemed to them strange that they were here. In their minds, every one of them felt they had the right to live the life of a *grand seigneur*.

"They are delightful, these people," said a short marquise.

"And to think, in twenty years their children will beat all of us to death," added Saint-Germain.

> *Demain donnons au diable*
> *un monde turbulent*

trilled the marquise, nervously. The people in the gallery were growing impatient. It seemed they were waiting for something that was taking too long to materialize. Meanwhile, the peasants allowed themselves a rough but restrained, sly exhilaration. Then six servants entered the hall and brought in slim, very tall carafes of a dark wine which was announced as the favorite drink of the voluptuary, King Charles VII. At this moment all of the nervous, impatient, tongue-in-cheek remarks in the gallery ceased. A boundless excitement possessed them all. They looked at one another as if colluding. Their eyes, especially those of the women, seemed to shine ecstatically. It was as if all of them were dazzled by a vision invisible to me. Everywhere around me was silent, surging excitement. If these people, who had to have planned something horrible, had now set upon one another with daggers I still would not have thought it the worst thing. Even more terrible things had to be prepared for. These people, jaded as they were by pleasures, seemed to know that something outrageous even to their minds would now come. Only the Count of Saint-Germain remained calm. Smiling, he approached me.

"What is going on here," I asked. "Where have you led me? Is this the revolution already?"

"Not for a while yet," he said mildly. "These good people have only been given a little aroph to drink."

Meanwhile, in the hall below, the black beverage was being poured into glasses. Some of the peasants had already begun drinking. Their eyes began to sparkle. At first they looked somewhat uncertain, as if they didn't believe their own feelings. Then they appeared to mutually encourage one another to do something. They still hesitated, but fury could erupt at any moment.

"This is the revolution!" I cried, horror-stricken. "These peasants will kill us. Saint-Germain is amusing himself at our expense; he would see us all on the guillotine."

My companions regarded me with the disgust and contempt they might ordinarily reserve for a theatergoer interrupting a tragedy by cracking nuts.

"This is the revolution!" I shouted once more.

"And what would it matter?" said the marquise, for whom my shouting had now become too much.

"Don't frighten them," said the count. "Incidentally, this is not the revolution."

One of the peasants suddenly grabbed his neighbor by the arm; the neighbor then broke into loud, sensual laughter. Everyone seemed to have been waiting for just this signal. The guarded, awkward people burst into uproarious, hooting laughter. They seemed to realize that up to this point each had secretly considered himself alone to be the lowest of beasts, and was now happily surprised to find that others were exactly the same. Every one of them, to the great astonishment of their neighbors, suddenly had the familiar desires forbidden by the church written all over their faces. They seemed to simultaneously discover the animal nature in one another. Each pressed himself greedily against the others; for the moment gender did not matter.

"You devil . . . You slut . . ." they shouted, and slammed against one another's bellies.

"As you can see, there is no danger here for us," whispered the count, smiling.

"I have to expose myself," cried a young peasant woman.

The hands of many men reached out for her and snatched away her clothes.

"Me too . . . me too!" came the confusion of cries.

They all abandoned their seats. The chairs fell over; tableware flew about; a demented cry arose from the milling crowd. Those in the gallery could no longer hold back their delight. The ladies shouted to the men below the way bullfighters are commonly encouraged in the arena. Some of the gentlemen drew their swords and threw them down with cries of "Blood . . . blood!"

In the midst of this general agitation a breathless black-bearded Capuchin monk suddenly pushed his way to the parapet rail.

"Oh life, glorious life," he shouted, enraptured. "I want to bathe in life!"

With these words he tore off his brown hair shirt. For a moment his naked, wiry form was seen on the balustrade, then with a quick leap he jumped down into the crowd. A nameless fury had seized the peasants. Only scraps of clothing still hung from the bloody bodies; the veins of the men were distended; the women who had yielded to the onslaught, insatiable, dug their fingers into the bodies lying next to them. Some wailed for death, so as to cure their insatiable frenzy. They took up shards of glass or china in order to blind or to kill themselves or others, laughing maniacally. Those in the gallery were so delighted they no longer knew what to try next. Whatever was in reach was thrown below: mirrors off the walls, champagne glasses, chairs; even the curtains were torn down and burning candles flung. Only the Count of Saint-Germain stood smiling in the midst of it all. Occasionally, he would speak: "I have seen more interesting things in fourteenth-century London."

But no one listened to him.

"Who has the courage to throw me down?" cried the short marquise. "My love to the man who dares!"

None of the gentlemen appeared to take her seriously. Suddenly the arms of the Capuchin rose from the throng in the hall.

"Come, little marquise, your great-grandmother was my first lover . . ."

"Gilles de Laval," cried the marquise, beside herself. "I recognize you . . . so like your abominable portrait . . ."

She tore off her clothes, jumped down, and disappeared with Gilles de Laval as if beneath the waves of the sea.

Gilles de Laval . . . ! The name had a fascination for the women. Suddenly they all wanted to emulate the marquise and shouted that they should be thrown down. As if compelled by some strange force, one man after another seized the lady next to him and threw her over the balustrade. For a few seconds, duchesses and marquises, the bearers of the finest names in France, could be seen flying naked through the air.

The women landed with bruised limbs. Dizzy, they tried to stand and limped around a little. All around them, however, the fire seemed to have gone out. A little embarrassed, they looked over the heaps of limbs and

broken tableware. They had no idea what to do. And yet just now they had felt so brave. Something quite mad had gone on, something into which they had wanted to plunge themselves. Now, when they had come down, it was all over. How gladly would these ladies have enjoyed some of the small pleasures of cruelty! Courage had indeed come to them too late. At times a hand in the spasm of death clawed or even stabbed at these delicate white bodies that moved about like miniature Valkyries on the field of battle. Occasionally, a finger even wounded them slightly, and then they emitted pretty, small cries of ecstasy, like well-bred children who, upon being washed in cold water, shivering, call out, "Whew . . . how warm!" The ladies sadly realized that they had come too late, and even now servants were coming into the hall with shovels. The naked marquises pressed themselves shamefaced into the corners and held their hands over their breasts and groins. The servants opened the windows and shoveled out the remains of the festivities. Out in the courtyard pale human bones that bore witness to Count Gilles de Laval's previous festive periods could be seen in the morning's first light. The marquises, however, crept sad and shamefaced out through a small side door. They regretted having behaved so ineptly. The poor ladies had stripped themselves bare for nothing.

In the gallery, those who remained behind had sunk into exhausted silence. They slowly caught their breaths. Some announced that it was time to depart and stood up. Handshakes were exchanged, appointments made for the following day. Some, indefatigable, wanted to go to supper. The Count of Saint-Germain, the man whom no one at all wanted to see leave, apologized, smiling. He had to return home, because he still wanted to translate a few chapters from the Akshara Para Brahma Yog before the night was over. No one ever raised objections to such excuses of the scholarly count, and so we took our leave of these polite people.

"Did you notice anything?" the count asked me once we were on the street.

"Many things," I replied.

"I mean, did you notice that I myself am Gilles de Laval? That is my name in the fifteenth century." He looked at me triumphantly.

"Impossible, you were in the gallery the entire time. You spoke of London . . ."

"For a moment, certainly, but can you remember seeing Gilles and me at the same time, even for a second?"

"No, but . . ."

"Now you see. Next time, I will invite you to a flagellants' procession in Italy."

He helped me into a carriage, where I immediately fell asleep.

When I again awoke—I felt as if I had slept longer than my entire previous life had lasted—a bowl of fruit stood before me. I very much wanted to grab it but couldn't find the strength to do so. Tears came to my eyes. I felt disgust for my own life, from whose miserable and mindless vortex I believed I had, as if by some miracle, escaped. These unreachable fruits would bring me recovery, unspoiled, easily fulfilled wishes in place of feverish cravings. Some well-meaning soul had dragged me back, somewhat roughly, from the edge of an abyss before which I had stood unaware.

"Do you know where you are now?" asked the smiling Alta-Carrara, who lay across from me on a divan.

There were several men in the room, talking. Some inquired after my health and gave me advice.

"You were there," I thought, "while I was pointlessly wasting my life in false sensations." Still, I was happy to discover entirely unfamiliar feelings in myself, something like remorse. I felt a bitter taste when I thought about my life, which had been based on a burning imagination and a feverishly disjointed intellect.

Someone must have guessed what I had wished, because I felt the cool tartness of an apple close to my lips. I bit into it and to me it was as if I scented fresh morning breezes all around me. I recognized the necessity of a new life—without the hateful frenzy, which was still in me. I longed for sober responsibilities. I was obliged to endure suffering, to frankly demand it of fate, which had cheated me out of the best in life by sparing me. I was almost ashamed. And at the same time I was excited about the rarity of such an emotion in a soul like mine.

Alta-Carrara, however, began speaking in a low voice:

CARNIVAL

"Thirty years ago, when I was still receiving my first lessons in the school of pleasure, some Venetian nobles once tried to revive a charming eighteenth-century Carnival custom. They gathered together in the open space of the Erberia in the final hour of the night, as the first bright glimmer appeared over the lagoon. It was considered very elegant to appear as ravaged as possible. People came in tattered fancy-dress costumes, limp flowers hung in the women's loose hair. The pale cheeks, the flickering eyes were meant to inform their fellows of ecstasies enjoyed within the past quarter-hour. We loved to arouse the envy and conjectures of the others, and to show that we knew how to laugh about it all. It scarcely needs to be stressed to the connoisseur of the human heart that many of the new arrivals had come not from the ballroom, nor from the gaming table, nor from concealed small rooms. Rather, they had just gotten out of bed, had carefully prepared their disheveled appearance, and

sacrificed their morning's sleep to fashion. I had spent the night in the Sala del Ridotto, danced a lot, gambled and drank. I was particularly drawn to a figure in a yellow silk mask. Her voice had a wonderfully warm, whispering tone. She knew how to cling softly, and her large white teeth gleamed under the edge of her mask. I was eighteen years old and was sure she was at the very least a duchess in disguise.

"Take me to the Erberia," she asked me toward morning, and with her I crossed the empty dark plaza. We mingled with the laughing couples wandering along the banks of the canal in the Erberia.

"Marchesina, I know you," called a passing masked figure.

"Only a marchesina," I thought.

"Where is Ersilia?" a passing Pierrette asked.

"Sick, very sick," replied my companion.

A number of barges that brought food for the market were berthed at the Erberia. A laughing courtesan paid a gold coin to a peasant from Chioggia for her steaming morning cabbage soup, the fragrance of which was sensually taken in by all the bystanders.

"I'm freezing," said my friend the Dolcisa. "Come home with me! I like you."

"Who are you?" I asked, nearly speechless with surprise. Until then I had had every reason to presume my companion to be a somewhat exuberant society lady.

"You are stupid," she said. Her dark eyes flashed beneath her mask. She drew me into a side street.

"Are you really a marchesina?" I asked, confused.

"Ridiculous; a nickname."

"Who is Ersilia?" I asked after a pause.

"Oh, poor sister Ersilia!" she sighed, but not very much moved. "She is going to die. She whispers with her saints and will not see what we do."

I was frightened, without giving any thought as to why.

"I'm a good girl," she went on. "I don't grant my love to everyone, but I am poor."

Now I believed I had something to seize upon. Her mild, frank innocence delighted me.

Cool morning air wafted around us. We walked silently through the dark lanes and crossed countless narrow canals. On no account would Dolcisa take a gondola. We met no one.

Eventually, as if stepping into a clearing, we entered a small square. In the corner glared a gloomy old palazzo. Dolcisa unlocked a wildly baroque little side gate and pushed me inside. All around us was a stifling darkness. We went up a number of creaking steps. We came to a standstill in front of a door.

"Wait for me here," she whispered. "Let me go into the room first and change my clothes."

She kissed me in the dark and went in through the door. I walked to a latticed window, through which the first light of dawn penetrated into the narrow landing. My eyes fell on a dilapidated, once certainly quite magnificent palace courtyard. Might she be a lady who wanted to have a secret carnival adventure? But these old crumbling palaces were often available for anyone to rent for next to nothing. Dolcisa left me waiting for a long while. "Perhaps she doesn't have the courage to call me in," I thought, and I quietly went into the room. It was as dark as it was outside. I heard a soft sigh come from the corner, and it sounded to me as if someone were rolling over on a bed.

"She's waiting for me," I told myself. "It is chivalrous to make the situation as easy as possible for her."

I went forward until I bumped into the bed where the woman lay. Under my kisses she moaned loudly, clawing at me and calling on the Madonna. This tremendous arousal frightened me. "Maybe she is from Naples," I reasoned. I already knew that the women of Venice loved differently, calmly sipping kisses. As so often happens in these quick adventures, a feeling of—I won't say aversion—of complete satiety in the moment after the pleasure came over me. An irresistible urge to be alone, to be in my own rooms, seized me, and it seemed to me that this completely ordinary feeling was today intensified immeasurably, as if I were a criminal overcome by horror at the scene of his crime. I jumped up; she did not hold me back. Because of the nature of our meeting, I thought myself entitled to press a few gold coins into her hand, which convulsively closed on them. I then hurried out. On the stairs I heard footsteps behind me.

"My love, come back," cried Dolcisa. "Why are you leaving?"

Two bare arms embraced me. A soft cheek rested against mine in the dark; youthful hot breath rushed over my face. Helpless, I let myself be drawn back up the stairs. Dolcisa led me through the room where I had earlier been, into a small antechamber. Very thin dawn light flowed in through a skylight. Black clothes hung on a chair and two fat straw-yellow candles were set out.

"They are for Ersilia, when she is dead," said Dolcisa. Her white chemise rippled with ghostly brightness.

"Could we have more light," I said, a little depressed.

"No, no. Everything here is plain and humble. We must live up here because the large rooms are so cold in winter. They should also be redone, but we have lost our money."

"Are you a marchesina?" I asked, again amazed.

"That needn't concern you. You are still such a child."

Had I hurt her? She went to the wall, where hung a colorful wax image of the Virgin Mary. A small oil lamp burned behind red glass in front of it. Its glow bathed the image in rosy light. Dolcisa blew it out.

"What are you doing?" I asked uneasily.

"So the Madonna doesn't see what we are doing."

Then she came to me. We sank onto a bed and this time I enjoyed the gentle, heavy, almost sluggish embrace of a Venetian woman.

Dolcisa was the first to rise. She went naked into the other room. She approached the bed where I had laid before and she thrust her hand under the sheets.

"Dead!" she suddenly cried with some horror. Helpless, she sank down onto her knees by the bed. The naked woman prayed in the dim morning light.

Startled, I jumped up. I lit one of the fat straw-yellow candles. Holding the light high, I stepped into the antechamber. As if paralyzed, I remained standing at the door as the flickering glow illuminated the bed. There, glassy-eyed, lay a splendid young woman, whose abundant dark hair billowed around her head like a mysterious cloud. She was very pale, of an unapproachable, solemn beauty, like an antique statue of a deity. Dolcisa knelt before her in hasty, rushing prayer.

"She's dead!" she cried, turning around, and there was something like genuine grief in the tear-hushed voice. "She wasn't a sinner like me. She died a virgin."

Shivering, I stepped closer. Dolcisa's gaze slipped back to the corpse, whose splendid white form lay half-bared before us.

"She was more beautiful than me," she sighed, and it appeared as if by making this sudden admission wished to make up for something she had failed to do while she was alive. She closed her sister's eyes and started to fold the stiffening arms over the body. Then she noticed a sparkle between the clenched fingers. She discovered the

gold coins. I could hardly remain standing, but Dolcisa let out a cry of joy.

"The Madonna was kind," she cried. "She answered my prayer. Now I can give my sister a decent burial."

Thankful, she returned to her prayers.

It was now light. I stood before the pair, uncertain. I asked Dolcisa if I could somehow be of service. But she said no and immediately sank again into fervent prayer. I left.

For two days I walked around as if deranged. Neither in my apartment nor in the street could I find peace at the thought that I had embraced the dead. On the third day I was seized by an uncontrollable curiosity. I sought out the neighborhood again, to learn something more about the inhabitants of the old palazzo. As I walked into the small square I saw a crowd that had gathered around the wide-open main gate of the palace. A priest and two choirboys came into the street. Then a black coffin was carried out. It was decorated with ornate silver flowers that were intended to lend it an impression of grandeur. It was loaded into a hired gondola and the few wreaths were stretched out as fully as possible. Dolcisa followed, sobbing in miserable yet dolled-up mourning. She boarded a second gondola, accompanied by a frail old gentleman of old-fashioned elegance who seemed very ill at ease. A few people boarded a third gondola and the funeral procession silently crept through the lagoons. Almost insensible, I looked on.

The whispering of the bystanders now rose to a live-ly chatter.

"The poor marchesinas," said an old woman. "And what a splendid life there once was at the palace, back when the old marchese was still alive . . ." "They were licentious," said a fat baker's wife. "No one wanted to have anything to do with them . . ." "No one can say any-thing against Ersilia," said a young man. "She was virtu-ous." Then several voices crowded against one another: ". . . Consumption, dying so slowly . . . poor, lonely Dol-cisa . . . still so young . . . but she has the old uncle . . . she will seek a more glamorous fate than just caring for him until he dies . . ."

Alta-Carrara's tale was at an end. Around me I saw and smelled old carved, worm-eaten wood. I listened as slow-ly decaying, centuries-old marble palaces, overgrown with moss, crumbled. The smell of mold hung over ev-erything; it was suffocating. The works of men could be heard crumbling through time. All around me the centu-ries rustled upward in murky vapors. Everything seemed to have suffered the kiss of death and was destined to decline. I had the vague feeling that I myself was guilty of the fact that the world should die. Oh, I had used my days badly. It could have been otherwise, had I wanted it to be so. How I rejoiced over the punishment coming to me. The suffering I had been waiting for began. I felt as though in the midst of the crumbling world something of great concern to me had tumbled down. As I glanced around it looked just like a booth at a fair, one with a purple-upholstered mirror before which candles burned, but inside which the major events of my life could be viewed through peepholes. It was embarrassing that so many people had peered in. That surprised me, as I had once been proud of my rich, colorful life.

"Go on . . . Go on," I cried. "More of this bittersweet wisdom." And as if from an abyss appeared a powerful-looking man. He had a blue-black square-cut beard, like an Assyrian magus, and was wrapped round with purple velvet, which he stroked like a beloved cat. He spoke apathetically, in an almost contemptuous tone that would later, however, rise to a violent excitation. He told this tale:

THE SIN AGAINST THE HOLY GHOST

In Spain there once was a group of young people who
were in search of something truly amusing. Everything
reminiscent of madness or the hospital was completely
foreign to them. They also despised the taking of intoxi-
cating drugs. These extremely feeble palliatives were then
not in keeping with the times. They also knew nothing of
spiritualism, the cesspool of mysticism, nor of hypnosis,
which, in our miracle-less time leaves the exact sciences
lagging behind. They felt that through the power of the
will alone—with assistance from humor, imagination,
courage, and finesse—that unprecedented spiritual dramas should be produced in others. Dramas that would
perhaps cast their shadows into the next world—a kind
of jesting with prospects of eternity. Unfortunately, the
list of mortal sins is completely exhausted almost daily
all around us. Here one kills his beloved, a deplorable sci-
ence awakens in another the arrogance of assuming the

likeness of the divine, a third gorges himself, and whatever other misdeeds unimaginative people might conjure. There is only one crime that the church assigns a special status by declaring it can never be forgiven. The priests even say that God scarcely allows it at all. This is the sin against the Holy Spirit. The young people I want to tell you about could therefore conceive of no more mysterious, more remarkable thing than the occurrence of this outrageous sin. Above all, they wanted to know whether it was at all possible, how it would take place, whether God would intervene, whether the world would stop turning, or if perhaps nothing at all would occur.

The sin against the Holy Spirit consists simply of insulting, of blaspheming against the Most Holy. There are three requirements: will, awareness, and the power of the blasphemer. He must *want* to commit the highest possible sacrilege, must *understand* whom he offends, and what he risks by doing so, therefore he must *have faith* that through the *power* of his will and his deeds he will be capable of striking God. His abuses should not bounce around like the barking of an angry little dog. Apart from Satan himself, who, as we know, was once the most beautiful of the angels and now is in continual revolt against the Holy Spirit, the sin can in fact only be committed by a saint who in the service of God has acquired the power of prayer, the faith that moves mountains, who suddenly turns against God.

First, a suitable victim was sought. There were a number of young women whose purity had performed miracles. But it turned out that their virtue was little more than the lack of opportunity to fall. If they felt God alive within themselves, Satan's tricks and wiles were almost entirely unknown to them.

Finally, they thought of fourteen-year-old Teresa Alicocca, the daughter of a courtesan. Since the birth of her child the mother had had no more terrifying thought than that she would follow a path similar to her own, and even if within herself there was nothing more to be corrupted, she nevertheless delivered the daughter to the strictest upbringing in a convent of Carmelite nuns. Nothing more would have been heard of her than of the other pupils, had she not at such an early age been consistently praised by the priests as a shining example of the miracle of *substitution*, in which Teresa's patron saint of the same name had famously excelled as well. With prayers and chastisements she had succeeded—through the intercession of Saint Teresa—in confronting evil in place of her mother, through *substitution*. She voluntarily confronted the demons of lust and greed that were intended for her mother. As this continued, despite her faith, she succumbed to the Satanic currents and allowed herself to be swept along. Henceforth Teresa knew how to navigate such effusions from Hell and how to overcome them. The upshot of this was that her mother—to her surprise—was suddenly able to keep the promises she had repeatedly made in the confessional. She began to lead a penitent's life and thanked heaven that from the fruit of her sin grace had been allowed to flower.

To the young people, no one could have appeared more suitable to their enterprise than Teresa Alicocca. She not only felt and saw God, but Satan's traps were also known to her, she who had never sinned. She no doubt possessed the power to commit the great sin. If she could be brought to it without intoxication she would also have the needed awareness. So it was only a matter of creating the third requirement within her: the will to blaspheme the Holy Spirit.

It was not difficult for the young people to approach Teresa, because there was a priest among them, Friar Tomás de León, who was secretly devoted to Satan. It was through him that they had come to know the details about Teresa. The air of piety which surrounded him, coupled with an uncommonly keen insight into the human soul, had prompted the Carmelites to choose him as their confessor.

He knew that people like Teresa are never content with themselves, that they repeatedly open recesses of their consciousness in which lie small reproaches, doubts, reminders of omissions. Sensible, benevolent priests are in the habit of temporarily banning such penitents from in-depth soul-searching. Friar Tomás, on the other hand, reinforced this self-tormenting voice, by asking Teresa whether she felt entirely free of the mortal sin of pride, whether she did not sometimes consider herself a saint because she even took the misdeeds of others on herself. Substitution is indeed one of the works pleasing to God, but was Teresa truly pure and humble enough? By daily putting his finger into this wound, at first so small, the priest succeeded in creating in Teresa an excruciating confusion.

Could the conversion of her mother not be seen as evidence of the purity of her prayers? she timidly dared to argue. What would it matter to the Evil One if a whore, one that he was sure of, lived modestly for a time when in exchange he could capture a virgin by way of the mortal sin of pride? Teresa became so insecure that for days on end she didn't dare practice substitution. She even asked God not to set her any more trials than he had intended for her in His righteous anger. When the priest saw her strength was thus broken, he asked her whether she had not in fact fallen into the opposite error? Whether she, who was perhaps indeed a chosen one, had renounced the miracle out of cowardice and lethargy, she who, out of sheer filial love, must do everything to save her mother's soul. Teresa wanted to try substitution again, but when she knelt before the Savior she felt that her anxious, broken prayers no longer had any power. An insane fear of the Devil gripped her, and tormented by her own sins she could no longer perform the miracle. She became more and more aware of her own impurity. Had she not sometimes exulted in being a woman because she could therefore more intimately love the Savior? She was even more of a prostitute than was her mother, who had succumbed to the weakness of the flesh and then, repentant, had fled to the Madonna. She however carried the baseness of her sex to the altar, mingled her lasciviousness with her prayers. Her ecstasies, which she had taken for a presentiment of eternal bliss, proved to be desecrations of God. The voices of the saints, which she believed she was hearing, were the flattering sounds of desires being indulged. She had sinned against the Holy Spirit. She confessed this state of mind to the priest, who, however, was still not at all satisfied with this success. He saw that the sin against the Holy Spirit existed for the time being only in Teresa's tormented imagination. He initially encouraged her in her error.

"These imperfect, sullied prayers," he explained, "are of course worse than confessed atheism. Open unbelief is barren, foolish, impotent. But such fevered prayers gain a certain power all the same, by way of the fervently aroused soul. They are not loud and powerful enough—as are the pure entreaties of the immaculate heart—to join with the eternally ascending current of prayer of Christianity and so continually link the supplicant with the common, invisible church that sustains and protects him, in the lap of which the temptations of Satan are of no concern. Such prayers, however, no doubt have the power to create streams which, repelled by the main current of prayer, return again to the supplicant, to enfold him with their impurity as if with hot hands, to darken his cell as if with cobwebs, to smother him under the larvae of his own unholy thoughts, until he suffocates in his sinfulness."

With this declaration Friar Tomás ensured that Teresa could no longer endure the solitude of her cell. Fleeting mirror images of her sins seemed to buzz about in the air. It was as if the webbing that the Evil One had wrapped around her was already so thick that even her most sincere prayers were no long able to slip through. She felt as if she were separated from the common invisible church. Taking advantage of this situation, the priest ordered Teresa to leave her cell. Satan has it in for cloisters in particular, and those where substitution is practiced are particular magnets for the Satanic presence. One with a weak nature, like Teresa, was therefore at all times better relegated to a secluded cloister cell. As father confessor he knew how to make her understand that it was their duty to keep such an extraordinary, disturbing case as hers from the gentle, serene mind of the Mother Superior, as it would cause her to fall into the greatest of confusion.

One night Teresa Alicocca left the cloister through a garden gate. Friar Tomás took her in a rowboat to the half-blind, half-deaf sexton of a remote, rarely visited church. There she would for a time replace the harmful tranquility of her previous life with the life of a lowly helping hand in a poor household. Nothing seemed more plausible to her than that through exhausting, humble labor she could gradually once again return her confused soul to peace. Friar Tomás visited her daily. He told Teresa that her mother had fallen back into her old life of sin. The old temptations that the daughter had protected her from now accosted her anew, and she was particularly susceptible to these shameful blasphemies because of her despair over the disappearance of her daughter. Friar Tomás brought similar news every day. Teresa would have very much liked to have rushed to her mother, but the priest knew how to restrain her. She would be found and brought back to the cloister. What further benefit to her mother would her presence bring? She would do better to regain her former purity by way of penance and prayer and—assuming a seemly humility—once again attempt the miracle of substitution. She at once exclaimed:

"If anyone has to fall victim to Satan, why can it not be me? I am much worse than my mother."

The priest looked at her searchingly for a long moment. The thought that he intended to gradually insert into her mind had now arisen spontaneously within her.

"What you desire, my daughter," he said quietly, "is possible. If you wish to pledge yourself to the Evil One in order to save your mother, he will accept that."

"I wish to," she responded tonelessly, and Friar Tomás de León dropped to his knees in front of her and kissed the floor.

"Blessed among women," he cried out. "Daughter of God, sister of Our Savior. Woe is me, the blind one, because I took you to be a sinner, because you *willingly* took on the *appearance* of greatest iniquity. But did not Nicodemus also at first doubt the deity of the Lord, because His was a mortal body? Behold, I am the first to fall down before you, unworthy as I am to loosen the straps of your shoes. Forgive me for not recognizing you."

Teresa had listened in the greatest confusion.

"Stand up," she said shakily. "What do you want of me? Do you want to tempt me; do you want to arouse the devil of pride in me anew?"

Friar Tomás stood:

"Behold, I am called to reveal to you one last shocking prophecy, which the church has until now kept the deepest of secrets.* Jesus Christ became a man; His redeeming arm stretched over the world right into purgatory, but His divinity stopped at the gates of perdition. The children of Hell remain unredeemed, because the only way to do this is to sin against the Holy Spirit, and that the Son of God cannot do. However—so it is said—in the last days a woman shall be born. She will voluntarily pass through the gates of Hell. She will not close herself off from her sinful humanity. She will freely choose to commit the greatest sin in order to release the shackles of those who believed their torment would be eternal. That is the final achievement of the benevolence of the Lord. But then she will repent and go to heaven. She must then force open the Trinity, now fulfilled, and she will be enthroned at the heads of God the Father, the

---

* Is it necessary to declare that the Church has never acknowledged anything of the kind?

Son, and the Holy Spirit, riding upon the dove, in an eternal unity of four."

Friar Tomás again fell to his knees.

"Stand up, stand up," cried Teresa. "I dare not believe you—I tremble at the idea of being a Chosen One—another will come. Only tell me—I implore you—what can I do to protect my mother from damnation?"

The priest rose.

"As Christ walked a span of time on Earth, so you will go to Hell to fulfill a period of damnation, and, along with the most impenitent of sinners, deliver yourself and your mother."

"How can I do that?" Teresa asked, trembling.

And Friar Tomás continued, relentlessly:

"Only one who is born of woman may obtain a physical body. Only one who commits the greatest of sins, that which can never be forgiven, will go to Hell."

"The sin against . . . ?" stammered Teresa.

"Yes, the sin that Christ could not commit, His divinity barred from Hell. Do you think that he deliberated about whether, when he became a man, he had to forfeit his divinity? And you are only putting your humanity at risk. Just as the impurity of the Conception was removed from Mary, so shall you not be defiled by your voluntary sin."

Friar Tomás left without waiting for an answer. Teresa lay in tears on the flagstones of the church the entire night, pleading for enlightenment. Was it a lack of humility if she sometimes wanted to rejoice that she perhaps was the Chosen One?

The next day Friar Tomás brought the news that Teresa's mother had been persuaded with gold by a company of young revelers to dance naked before them as Salome. They wanted to have a head of John the Baptist made for her out of wax, but she, who for a week now had been unable to refrain from blasphemies, had secretly given the order for the wax to be cast not in John's visage, but rather with the well-known features of the thorn-crowned Christ in the Chapel of Saint Ignazia. She was said to have shouted why had God taken away her daughter with her powerful prayers, now it was *His* fault if she gave herself to Satan. Undoubtedly—said the priest—she intends a dreadful desecration of Jesus' head, the sin against the Holy Spirit.

Teresa fell helpless to the floor.

"Do you recognize a sign from God, my daughter?" said Friar Tomás. "Does He not Himself remind you that the hour has now come when you shall voluntarily take your mother's sin upon yourself, when you alone shall open Hell, so that it will never again be closed once you have redeemed all of the damned?"

"I don't understand you."

"Do you think that God often permits this sin? Today, at the moment when you shall fulfill your vocation, He will permit it to transpire in one close to you, in your mother, whom you are already accustomed to representing before the Evil One. Need more threads meet in a knot? The vices of your mother, your desire to save her, were only signs for your grand work. Seldom is God's will so clearly revealed. On that dangerous evening I will immerse your mother in sleep with a potion. You, however, having donned the jewelry amassed by the richest young men of the city, will perform the dance. *You will dance the sins of perdition:* arrogance, drunkenness, animal lust—you who are humble, sober, and chaste. You will voluntarily curse God, spit on the head of Christ and, in heat, laughing with lust, implore Satan for eternal damnation. At that, the gates of Hell will open before you and you may bring forth all of the damned— your mother among them—into heaven."

Teresa twisted despairingly on the floor, while this foretaste of the coming spectacle aroused the priest to the point of dizziness.

"So, you will take on all of the anticipated sins of the future through the greatest that can ever be committed. However, in the moment when Satan lustfully stretches out his arm for you, to raise you up as the Queen of Hell, he is beaten in his own lair, caught in his own net, because through your human body God will have deigned, this one terrible time, to use deception—the embodiment of which is Satan. So—as a final mystery—the devil will be destroyed by his own ways, the deceiver deceived, and sin shall be dead forever. That, however, shall be the work of the saintly Teresa Alicocca, and the heavenly host who carry her aloft will sing: *Gloria patri et filiae.*"

Friar Tomás crossed himself and left her alone.

He knew she now was prepared enough that she could be taken by surprise at the last minute.

On one of the following nights Teresa Alicocca lay, as was her habit, before the altar in the small dark church, outstretched in supplication. Her loud sobbing in the darkness was suddenly interrupted as the organ, as if by ghostly hands, began to quietly play, and two fragile children's voices brightly and delicately sang "*Gloria patri et filiae.*"

A violent trembling came over Teresa. She believed it a miracle of illumination, and passionate prayers of thanksgiving flowed from her lips. Then Friar Tomás de León stepped from behind the altar with a candle in his hand. He was dressed in silvery white. Under his arm he carried a reliquary.

"Arise, Blessed One!" he called to her. "Let this lowest of servants adorn your body for the sacrifice!"

And the bright children's voices resounded light and clear through the vaulting.

"Arise, daughter of God, sister of Jesus!"

With no will of her own, blinded by the light which flowed around the priest, she rose. With gentle, agile hands he helped her to open her miserable cloister robe. It dropped down around her, like the physical remains of one transfigured. Her eyes fixed ardently on Christ, she sought to suppress her shame as if it were a pain. Her last garments fell. The priest gently drew off the rough shirt and laid his hands on the naked woman in blessing. He then opened the reliquary and took out sparkling jewels. "Don the sensuousness of the pearl-gray cloudy day, pregnant with sin, the burden of our treacherous craving!" He placed a pale, seven-fold string of pearls around her neck. "Let yourself be wound around with the gold-flecked blue of the sky, from the rejoicing of the creature that excites men to their colorful dance of Baal of their idolatrous art."

The priest wound a light blue satin ribbon with gaudy sun-colored topazes under her breasts, which stood out pointed and firm.

"Let yourself wander lustfully in balmy forests, sanctuaries of lust, of the effervescent waters shining in rainbows, where animals doze, siblings of the most sultry desires!"

Like leaves of forest foliage he spread deep fir-green emerald, smooth beryl, birch-pale chalcedony; moss-green nephrite and enticingly iridescent opals rested upon her hips.

"Bow down to the all-consuming fire that has burst the bowels of the Earth, ignited rebellion in the loins of the people!"

Unrestrained, prodigal, greedy, he encircled her with bracelets of blazing ruby and soft red carnelian;

garnets, almandines, and coral fell like drops of blood onto the groin of the virgin.

"Run your hands through your curls, that ocean, that burst of fragrance of your entangled desires; bear therein the will-o'-the-wisp of knowledge that hovers over the swamp of the senses, the eternal light that is the pride of the knowing ones!"

With wild fingers Friar Tomás loosened her billowing hair and pushed a diamond crown into it. Drunk on his own sparkling words, he said:

"Flaunt your nakedness, shine, sing your body forth amidst the finery and the sins with which Satan would mark you." But, as if in sudden despairing resignation, he went on: "Your steps will be weighed down by the sinister malediction of our crimson rutting nights, as the breath of Hell hisses incandescent in our faces, sparkling in perpetual rebellion and lust, in the cry for the light eternal!"

And Friar Tomás de León placed cloudy amethyst, night-dark sapphire, and aquamarine in dark-bluish strings on her from her flanks to her ankles like diaphanous oriental leg coverings.

Encumbered with all this splendor, with all the iniquities of the world, the fourteen-year-old stared at the Christ above the altar and knew not what was happening to her. Friar Tomás handed her the greenish, shimmering wax head of Jesus on a golden platter. He then took her by the hand and led her toward the church, which, meanwhile, was shining with brilliant candlelight. A white carpet was stretched out on the tiles. At its corners torches burned and bowls of myrrh steamed. Friar Tomás led the hesitant girl to the center of the carpet.

"Dance, daughter of Heaven, dance the dance of deliverance, and in this one single hour perform in boastful lewdness all the iniquities that Satan will yet demand of mankind!"

The organ suddenly fell into a wild rhythm. In the dimly lit corners of the church masked men struck holy vessels against one another like tam-tams and cymbals. The barbaric noise of tambourines rang out in abominable harmony with the festivities. Drunken screams of women came from behind the undulating curtains of the confessionals.

"Dance, dance!" cried the priest impatiently, and with leaping steps of his own appeared to be trying to encourage the hesitant one, who scarcely dared to move under the burden of the ornaments. And slowly, with shy movements, laden with the iniquities of the world, Teresa moved across the carpet, carrying the head of the Savior on a tray. The young people, the priest's friends, now suddenly sprang out from the corners, where men and women greedily crowded together. They danced joyfully around the carpet, carrying torches and naked swords.

"Wilder, madder," he shouted to the anxious one. "You must redeem us all. But our sins are still more burning, more shocking, more rapacious than your dance. You must dance more wickedly than are our iniquities, which scream to heaven. Only then can you dance us to redemption."

As the fury of the organ thundered down, Teresa was compelled to wilder and wilder dancing. She flung away the platter with the head and in sudden inspiration found within herself the Asian dancers' pensive, articulated turns of limb. She presented her open sex to the bright candles and, with a violent gesture, tore away the flower of her virginity, so that her white body bled on the red rubies.

"A bloody host of Satan!" Friar Tomás cried ecstatically. But she howled in pain and lunged at the wax head at her feet, embraced it like the head of a dancer, sank her teeth into it to stifle her pain.

And she danced the sins of Hell!

"Kiss him," the priest called to her. Helpless, she now did everything he commanded. "Mock him, spit on him, throw him down, dance over him, trample him, crush him—blaspheme the Trinity—call out to Satan!"

And Teresa Alicocca, bent under the weight of the sins of perdition, cried out, "Satan, Lucifer, Adonai!"

"What do you want?" cried a muffled voice from the crypt.

"Accept me into eternal torment!" moaned Teresa.

"And God—do you believe in Him?"

"I believe in Him, I feel His majesty, but still I call out to be free of Him—I want to be *yours*!"

"Are you willing to insult the Holy Spirit?"

"Haven't I already done that?"

"Do you want to be Lucifer's concubine who knows God and therefore hates Him?"

"I behold God," Teresa cried ecstatically, "and still I want to be your whore, Satan!"

At this moment the young people, armed with daggers, leapt onto the carpet.

"Hurry . . . hurry . . ." cried Friar Tomás, "before she can repent, before she destroys the great work!"

And in an instant they fell on the rapt woman dancing there. Six daggers were plunged into Teresa's body—into the heart, into the neck, into the belly, into the flanks, into the vulva—*but none appeared able to wound her.* Uncaring, she danced on, like a somnambulist. Six daggers bristled from her body as if they were part of her gaudy adornments.

"She feels nothing," one of the young people exclaimed, startled. He cut into the arm of the dancer with a knife, and no blood flowed. The daggers slowly fell from her like ripe fruit.

Life seemed to stand still in the moment of unfettered discharge. The brimming intoxication suddenly flew out of their souls. Empty—fragile—the disillusioned ones stood there and in their suddenly frozen minds scarcely knew how to pull back the reins of the flown phantom that had presently seemed like life.

They were too ashamed to speak; they felt how feeble their voices would now sound.

Moaning and wailing tore them from their stupor. They looked on in horror as Friar Tomás de León writhed on the floor. His eyes bored into the crucifix clutched in his hands, and he was screaming. They begged him for an explanation. But he didn't dare look up, to turn his eyes away from the Crucified One. With his hand pointing to the ceiling he bawled like a whipped animal: "God . . . God . . . !"

He bellowed the name of God through the vaulting.

"*God won't allow the sin against the Holy Spirit to come to pass.*

"While her body was the vessel for our filth, the Eternal One held her soul fast and made her life invulnerable . . . !"

It was as if someone whipped the young people on the backs of their knees and forced them to drop down.

Lying on the floor they whimpered pitiful prayers. Teresa staggered more and more slowly, her head fallen forward, her arms limp, and she sank down, like the flames of the candles around her that had burned down. From the corners of the dark church, however, from behind the curtains of the confessionals, from the white carpet, rose desperate moans and prayers of contrition.

The abyss of my life had opened so wide that it was possible for me to see down to the bottom. Where I had supposed infinitude I saw a limit. The human imagination, the play of reason, appeared to be exhausted; it could not be driven any further. For me it was as if on the path to knowledge my forehead came up against a dark wall, one that would not yield, however much I pushed against it. Could I ask for clearer evidence that I was on the wrong path, that I had lost my way? And I turned back around.

THE MESSAGE

I was walking in the streets of the city where I lived. I was conscious that I was approaching my apartment . . . Oh, yes, I had taken hashish. But where had my intoxication gone? I felt calm and content. Now I was on my way home. I never enjoyed hashish or opium there. You never know what parts of the fantasies will linger in the furniture. My room must remain pure. There I received a woman I loved; there I worked; sometimes friends came. Everything there was to my taste; I had purchased every object somewhere with conscious design . . . or it was a gift . . . or an heirloom . . . my entire life story clung to this furniture, as did my travels . . . a journal of sorts. It began with a cradle; then moved on to my toys; then came an old chair on which in evenings past my father had sat and told stories . . . and so it continued. There was a lamp, by the light of which I had prepared myself for an examination, and now even the photographs and pictures. And there was an old Chinese inkstand that my first love, in a fit of adorable anger, had broken and at a later time a clever boy had put back together. Everything in this apartment was alive. And I should allow random hashish fantasies to invade it? I had often refused to hold séances there. Nothing strange crosses my threshold! I was actually very happy to have such a refuge in the unclean life of this century.

I was just about to cross a street when I felt myself being nudged by a prostitute in an absolutely crude manner. She was elderly and fat. Her lips were frozen in that smile that looks like the petrification of a feeling feigned from the very beginning. While the assured, expert eyes of others of her kind can immediately distinguish one unsuitable for their purpose and be on their way, this one absolutely did not want to let me go. Despite my emphatic resistance she continued to press herself on me and to harangue me. Her flaccid cheeks were absolutely overburdened with makeup. It struck me that the protracted sordidness of this doll-like face was not capable of conveying the slightest expression, not even a particularly vicious or depraved one. Without replying, I continued on, but I could not get her out of my thoughts. What manner of men could possibly go with her? This non-entity didn't even have the appeal of filth, of foulness. What an absurdity—to offer such to someone! How could anyone come to occupy himself with her? She must have become a prostitute by chance, without revulsion, without preference, the same way most people choose their profession, a petite bourgeoise of the demimonde, a body that mechanically functioned as a woman.

"That is death," I thought, and instinctively quickened my pace, to get back home. The creature had disappeared or, more likely it seemed to me, had dispersed into the air and now pervaded every street, hung over the houses, over the trees, over the few people I encountered in the first light of dawn. The Parisian streets, whose natural, easy elegance I had otherwise enjoyed, suddenly seemed to me indifferent, stupid. The people I encountered seemed almost mindless: all of them pale and exhausted. For what reason? From some pleasure, perhaps? They didn't look like that at all. They just go to bed in the first light of morning, have mistresses who don't love them, pay more for everything than it is worth, get sick, go mad, fall into poverty. Why? No one knew why, they themselves least of all. A number of prostitutes scurried dolefully past me. They were bleary eyed, barely looked around. Then I again thought of the first, who had accosted me. She was futility personified, the imbecility of this entire stupid city life. I was tired and looked forward to sleep as I arrived home. At the moment I was about to slam the door, someone slipped in behind me.

"Incubus," murmured a voice. From that moment on I felt as if I were not directing my own actions. I was being pushed from outside. A paralysis, like that which comes over us in dreams, stopped me from showing the intruder the door or calling the concierge. I was pushed up the stairs from behind until I stood in front of the door of my study. As I did every night, I mechanically lit the lamp. Then I sank exhausted onto the chaise longue. The creature sat down across from me. I recognized the same prostitute who had first blocked my way on the street. The mindless misery that had settled on my nerves outside had now stepped into my room.

She sought, offering reason after reason, to persuade me that she should stay and that I had to give her a good donation. I don't know whether I answered at all. She, without much conviction, chided me for my depressed turn of mind, and then again, with absurd flattering words, sought to gain my favor.

". . . Don't act like a child," she said. "You know we all have to continue to have these kinds of dealings with death. In this the weak-willed one has a powerful master, the ambitious one a jealous rival, the egoist an evil child. You should have one lover warm her with your blood. Each according to his temperament or to his sins, if I may put it in a slightly old-fashioned way. Just think about the friends you spent the evening with. Do you think that they will not find an uninvited guest back home, one who demands from them a reckoning, promises, renouncements—the devil knows what. Until now you have inexplicably been forgotten. Now I come here to demand the levy of inner affliction that you owe to death in exchange for it letting you continue to live. So as not to frighten you, I approached you outside. You see how I sweeten the pill for you. If I had wanted, you just as easily could have found me sitting on your bed. Imagine for a moment how surprised you would have been in that case." She laughed raucously. "You see, I can be borne quite comfortably. Also, jealousy is foreign to me. You know, you are still a child, because today for the first time you are knowingly receiving a visit of this kind. Tomorrow you will no longer be a child. Just pay attention to how differently, how much more kindred to you people will be tomorrow. Half of your arrogance will be gone. And they will trust you more, because up until now they have felt that you know nothing of death. Isn't that so? That will now change. Now you have at least something in common with them." She looked around the room. "By the way, without you recognizing them, many messengers of death like me must have already come through here to have produced this pervasive smell of corpses."

"None, you damned animal." I shouted at her. "You are the first that has fouled these rooms."

But the hollow voice rattled on inexorably. My only hope was that it was all only a dream.

"Your crimes are actually fairly harmless. I hardly need even mention them . . . childishness! Because of it you continue to be spared the many dreadful visits that at night torment the moral cowards of the bourgeois, well-fed professionals and the money men. Sometime

I'll even tell you what they experience at night. Anyway, you know, we can chat together quite pleasantly. Your sort really are the most amusing kind for death to enter into a relationship with. Incidentally, one thing before I forget: You need not fear dying, not for a long while yet. My visit has not the slightest thing to do with that. I only bring the message that, for you, the first, thoughtless joys of youth are now finished."

Her voice had gradually grown a little warmer. She seemed to feel sorry for me.

". . . Are you still afraid of me? Do you know, then, who the others were, those you knew not the slightest about, who you once brought into your home at midnight and lay next to you like a good old lover? Did you perhaps know where they came from and where they went? Did you know which coffin was their daytime lodging before they came to you and after they left you? Did you ever once follow them in the morning? You know nothing about them, and yet you had no fear. And now you are frightened of me? How am I different from them? Do you know me to be less good, or more evil?"

"I tell you, none have crossed this threshold."

She burst into frightful, though not very loud, rough laughter.

"You are a sophist, my friend. You know full well that I speak not of flesh and blood . . . Think, for a moment, about your fantasies, your most secret thoughts. They hang on all the furnishings here like cobwebs. It is ridiculous to try to lie to me about anything. I know who you lie down with, who you entertain yourself with here for entire afternoons. Maybe you want the pleasure of having me seduce you like some young lad? You're too old for that and I'm too smart. I think we would be better off behaving like old friends, without lying to one another about anything."

I watched as she stood and put wood into the fireplace as if it were her own hearth. In front of the fire she undressed and cast her tattered clothing onto the floor. I closed my eyes when I saw the spongy, slack body. Then I must have fallen asleep.

When I awoke, the pale winter morning was shining into my room. I was surprised to find myself in my suit on the chaise longue in my study. The dirty clothes lying all around suddenly called the night's incident back into my memory. I jumped up and hurried to the door of the adjoining bedroom. There the fat, ashen woman lay in my bed. A bare arm hung down to the floor as if dead; the open mouth wheezed. An indescribable anger welled up inside me. I wrenched her from slumber. Half asleep, she called me a name from the street and grumbled because I had awakened her so early.

"Get out ... Go ... ," I cried.

Half angry, half surprised, she dressed herself with sluggish spite. She continually answered my urgings with rude, petulant phrases. It made me almost happy when I heard her complain that way. It was at least understandable. I had torn her from sleep and she complained—good. That was fitting, that was logical. But everything else was quite incomprehensible: that she was here, that she was in my bed.

I was finally about to push her out the door. But you should have seen her then: wounded to her core, almost paralyzed with petrifying astonishment, she shouted: "And the twenty francs . . . Well? . . . Didn't you promise me? . . . You filthy fellow . . . Maybe you believe that I just took a shine to your face . . . ?"

No sooner did she have the coin in her hand than she turned to flattery: "Don't be mad, my little wolf, I didn't know . . ."

She left. I dropped down in a half-faint.

I reflected on where and in what age I actually found myself.

I stepped in front of the large mirror above the mantelpiece. The entire room was reflected in it, but I did not see myself. I tapped on the glass, I felt my head, my limbs; they felt as they always had. But their fleshly appearance was gone.

"That woman has taken it with her, she has stolen me," I cried out. "This is madness. What sort of dens will it now drag me through?"

I suddenly grew calmer, because it came to me that this mirror was still in the year 189*, since which, after all, many years must have passed. How much had I experienced since then! No wonder I didn't see myself in it. But then came a new tormenting thought. I knew no one in this new period. I suddenly thought of the Count of Saint-Germain, who lived in all times simultaneously. He was actually to blame for everything. Moreover, he had said that I should visit him. From my window I whistled for a cabby, to travel to the count. I rushed down the stairs.

I rode on and on, relentlessly, for days, weeks, years.

In the Bois de Boulogne I got out. As if it had to be thus, I went to a bench on which I often used to rest in quiet hours, which from time to time would briefly interrupt my restless existence. A mild winter sun shone through the leafless grove. I don't know how long I sat there dreaming. I slowly recovered from the nocturnal visit. The explanation was that I had admitted this creature while intoxicated with hashish. But I felt a strong reluctance at the thought of having to enter my apartment again. There was something there with which I wanted to have absolutely nothing more to do. Strange knowledge had come to me that night. Where should I go now? Leave Paris, preferably leave Europe, for some farm on virgin soil. Then I thought it strange that I—I of all people—should feel something like this. It almost seemed to me as if I hadn't been intoxicated at all. The disembodied lover who is not a woman, rather the pretext for our dreams—the bacchanal of the most furious self-destruction—the embrace of death—the lascivious touching and stalking of the saint—had I really only

dreamed all of that? Somewhere I had experienced something similar, had done something similar. But where? When had it happened? I felt that I would have to give it a lot of thought. I knew only one thing for certain: I had recovered from a terrible illness that had allowed me to look death in the face. But for now, what to do with this new lease on life?

SMUGGLERS' PASS

*A Pre-Revolutionary Episode from the Private
Notes of a Journalist*

For half a century I have been silent about myself; I have been a mouthpiece for others. Today I am seventy-five years old. Therefore it is high time that I report an experience, if it is to be reported at all.

Twice I have traveled around the world; three times I have seen the midnight sun. In America I was aboard sailing ships four times, on steamships sixteen times; railroads have taken me from Cape Finisterre to the Yellow Sea free of charge; I have dined with two emperors, eleven kings, four chiefs, a Cassock commander, an Ottoman governor, a Great Khan, and two hundred and fourteen ministers. The Bey of Tunis awarded me his Order of the Sun, though my sovereign didn't allow me to wear it because with all its stars and ribbons it covered more than three-quarters of a medium-sized person, thus making a stronger impression on the uninitiated than the Order of the Black Eagle, and that would not do. Heinrich Heine has personally spoken divine crudities to me; Fanny Elssler almost loved me; Napoleon III listened with a gracious smile to my financial plans for the rescue of France. I have been a witness at one hundred and thirteen executions (the last was electric); I have publicly attested to the double-headedness, inordinate hairiness, or scientific importance of their freaks for more than two hundred financially needy mothers. I have known drunken kings, honest prostitutes, and modest tenors. I should have been scalped in Louisiana, been whipped in Tibet, but my elegant appearance saved me. I am fluent in no languages, but half or three-quarters so in thirty-six; my pronunciation of all of them is excellent. When it comes to words I am like the Norse god Heimdallr, who was born of nine mothers (and therefore must have had a nine-fold natural wit), needed less sleep than a bird, saw one hundred miles further at night than he did by day, and heard the grass growing on the ground and the wool growing on the sheep.

But I will tell you nothing of any of this today, you ladies of the province who find me to be an interesting man. Rather, I will report what I encountered during the last night before this eventful half-century began, and thereby leaf back through the pulp-paper pages of the book of my life.

I had a meager monthly pension of fifty guilders. (I later knew months in which, by the grace of God, I was able to bring in five thousand.) This and a malevolent restlessness in my mind dictated that I should become a poet. As befits this profession, I lived in a garret overlooking an ancient courtyard and countless gabled roofs, on which pairs of cats danced in the moonlight while in the dark corners of the rickety buildings the young women of the house held awkward conversations with their lovers. The moonbeams, however, were like strings stretched in the frame of my window, and my overflowing heart, as if it were a harp, played my longing to the sky. At times a girl visited me. She was not beautiful. (Poets' lovers are never beautiful, because those whose imagination forges gold crowns from blonde hair must overlook so much of reality that a few especially ugly features, such as hairiness, are unimportant, and he who makes the leap from eyes to stars doesn't need to leap very much further if those eyes squint.) Oh, Manolitha, called Marie, had rather coarse, unkempt hair, which I never noticed, and eyes slightly crossed. But she was also a woman whose physical features were *feminini generis*, like Venus and Mary. In her, my imagination had a springboard into the mystery of the always contentious and always complementary halves of the world, the eternal male and the eternal female. For this purpose Manolitha was enough, just as my garret was good enough for poetry. The poor child didn't know what was happening to her. She probably thought, This is how men are.

The town in which I lived lay not far from the border. Manolitha worked as a servant in the last house on the cliff road, which rose up over a lake. The road led into the neighboring country. One moonlit night—to me it seems as if all the nights at that time were moonlit nights—I had taken Manolitha to her door. I stood alone, high above the lake. The lights of the town glittered far away. The cliff wall stretched all along the road, fissured and frequently rent by noisy torrents. Formless dark cloud shadows wandered over the almost sun-bright lake. Here and there a fishing boat floated on the surface, its occupant plying his silent trade by lantern light. My lips still burned with the kisses of my beloved, which now, in memory, seem to have actually been a bit too modest. (By Heimdallr, the God of Journalism, I later loved some truly different women.) I hurried forward along the cliff road, on into the distance, to the south, with a vague yearning to receive from the silvery arms of this night of my youth the ideas, the words that would make me immortal. Half drunk, I wandered on and on. After a short time the cliff road curved away to the right into a row of clefts. A path barely a foot wide was carved into the wall that towered over the lake: the smugglers' pass. I felt as if I were facing something decisive about my life. To the right the path led to the cliff-enclosed darkness of the spruce wood past the mysterious waterfalls; to the left was the breakneck trail into the moonlight high over the broad flood below. I decided to go left, and as if on a thin wire I felt like I was walking freely in the light while I, mocking the danger, laboriously crept along above the abyss. I was amused at the thought that I might encounter a heavily laden smuggler on the narrow path, and I was curious about what would happen then. One of us would have to either turn back or plunge into the depths. It seemed to me that the path stretched on infinitely. As I could no longer see the starting point because of the bends in the path, nor beyond each projecting rock before me to any expected destination, I continued on with that almost eerie pedantry that often compels us forward simply so we don't have to go back on the same path, even if it sends us to our death. Unaccustomed to physical exertion I soon felt an almost unbearable fatigue. With my hands hurting at every contact with the rock, my self-control failing, a tremor in my legs warned of an approaching bout of vertigo. The lake was below me, nearly white; a fantastic false daylight trembled through the air . . . I can no longer recall the following period of time with any certainty. Had I plunged into the depths and beneath the tide into a fairy kingdom where our world is mimicked in a jesting masquerade, and do I still find myself in that Mummenschanz today? Or did I continue on with such supernatural effort that nothing more of my energies remained to spare for the activity of consciousness? In short, my memories at this point feel as if they are broken into two existences; a hole, a gap, divides this side from that side. I imagine that many people have such a gap in their existence that they seek in vain to fill. Either they take this lack seriously, dwell on it incessantly and so go mad, or they numb themselves as I do, with work and amusements and by similarly narcotic means. That is, they detour around their own lives.

My memory picks up again with the following situation: I am sitting on the floor in a completely closed room decorated with pelts and hanging fabrics. In front of me is a fire of brushwood that casts a glow on a circle of men with wild beards. On their belts I see the glimmer of richly decorated daggers. Their rough, scruffy limbs are clad half in rags, half in magnificent oriental coverings. These are obviously smugglers.—As I turned my eyes upward I saw the starry sky above me. We were in a roofless room; the walls were rock. Dark tunnels appeared to open from each of the square room's four corners. In front of the smugglers, and also in front of me, were expensive but chipped and broken plates and glasses set with food and drink that looked more appetizing than the scene would have led me to hope. They apparently had been waiting for me to awaken to begin the meal. I was very hungry and helped myself. They particularly encouraged me to drink. They were very courteous and obliging. An old woman who was addressed as "Bones" served us something she had apparently cooked herself. I would have liked to have asked how I came to be here, and who these people were, but I was afraid I would reveal my ignorance if I did so. (Incidentally, to allow no unwarranted expectations to arise in the reader, I note at this point that I never found out.) I made every effort to conceal the lengthy gap in my memory. After we had dined and I, without being drunk, found myself in after-dinner high spirits, my hosts proposed that they show me their dwelling in which, so they said, the best and most curious of Earth's treasures were stockpiled. Carrying torches, we walked into one of the tunnels, in which the walls were broken by iron doors.

"It's impossible for us to show you everything," one of them said. "But you will at least be able to form an idea of our collection."

They opened the first door. I will not tire you with a description of the expensive and curious things in the rock chambers. The articles I sent to the *** newspaper from around the world over the next fifty years provide considerable testimony about them. Just a quick overview: I saw the evening splendor of the desert, the stark blubber subsistence of the Eskimos; I saw Bayreuth with Norse gods once again come to life, with the riches of both worlds crowded around. (I should note that this occurred in the forties, before anyone had thought about Bayreuth.) I saw the battlefields of the Franco-Prussian war, but I discovered even more: incarnated ideas that had been forced into temporary or lifelong retirement; ideas to uplift mankind and world-destroying ideas lay on exquisite cushions; communistic systems sat amiably around tea tables; revolutions wallowed, growling, on their chains; poets' dreams went about in fabulous nudity—rather brazenly, I must confess—between upstanding, if poorly dressed, old bureaucratic crones. Hopes, ever hopeful, called out to women in childbirth who had been denied them; some new vices seemed pleasant from afar, but smelled bad close-up, which is why I did not bother to properly memorize their forms. Syphilis, a beauty, grieved because she was not allowed near vice-ridden Assyrian kings, but fate, for which the smugglers appeared to have enormous respect, did not want it that way, they assured me. *Idée fixes* crowded around unashamedly, as well. These were the only ones I had to have harsh words with—with one, who wore a laurel wreath, I even had to use my fists. Otherwise, the passions and the mortal sins behaved well, if also somewhat embarrassed, like coarse people who submit themselves to the constraints of a salon in order to be able to hold themselves harmless elsewhere later.

You can imagine the astonishment I felt as I walked about among these curiosities, but my astonishment grew when one of my companions, flattered by the pleasure I found in the collections, courteously invited me to pick out something that I particularly liked from the things I'd seen. I let my gaze wander indecisively. Again the *idée fixes* rudely pressed forward. But I made my way to a door standing half-open, revealing a shimmering red chamber in which—although it was not large—five hundred (so I was told) magnificent naked women were encamped. They were smiling silently to themselves, as if to say, We don't need to press forward, you will come to us. I was blinded by the white glow of their bodies. I had only seen such forms before in cast plaster and I thought, From now on real women will be even more ugly, though a real poet chooses to ignore it. The smugglers were obviously delighted by my confusion, which I was at first particularly thrown into by the burning glances of the one closest to me.

"I want these . . . all five hundred," I called out greedily, and was immediately very embarrassed.

Nothing could be easier, they answered merrily, and added that I should choose a second time—. They opened another door before me, through which shone an intense yellow light. It hurt my eyes. When I had become accustomed to it I saw that the walls, the floor, and the ceiling of the open chamber were paved with embossed gold pieces. I wanted to go further.

"There are around a million," they said.

"So?" I replied, indifferent, now glancing back into the chamber of the five hundred women, now sweeping my eyes searchingly over the other valuables all about me.

"It's a million," the smugglers repeated, astonished. "Don't you want it . . . ?"

"Oh no, I'd prefer the desert with camels and oases or something romantic like that . . ."

"You are a fool, sir. First you accept five hundred women, and now you spurn a paltry little million. What are you going to with your women without money? Do you believe they will leave you in peace? This crowd will all want gifts of jewelry and clothes . . ."

"But I very much prefer them naked."

"The women don't care about that: if you give them nothing, they will soon accept gifts from others."

I was very frightened by these words, and I quietly agreed to take the million. The smugglers were very happy and said that I could now choose one last time. This time they didn't want to influence me, they said, but they did very much wish to first show me something that was sure to please me mightily. They pushed open a jib door.

It opened without a key while all the other portals were made of iron and had heavy locks. This door, on the other hand, was so artfully concealed that only an initiate could find it. We went into a room, which had obviously never been put in order. A heap of metaphors, anaphora, symbols, allegories, newly minted figures of speech, citations, proverbs, jokes left to rot, all lay about helter-skelter. Poetic images and analogies hung on the wall in heavy frames in no apparent order. Perplexing tropes and metonymies peered out confusedly between them. Around the four walls of the room near the ceiling ran a wall shelf on which, between a small parlor stove, flasks, retorts, and other apparatus of the black arts, stood tall jars full of liquid. In these, like animals in alcohol, lay ideas, very good ideas, all of which were in a state of slow dissolution. Some were still clearly recognizable and had tinted the surrounding liquid only slightly; others were already formless, had become gelatinous, while the fluid appeared murkier and cloudier. In a few scattered jars there was nothing but formless, discolored slurry.

When I asked what these dilutions of ideas signified, the smugglers would give me no real answer. I would understand it someday, and if not, so much the better for me. I must confess that this seemed suspicious to me. I was involuntarily reminded of the kitchen at the inn, where a few pounds of meat may become as much broth as there is water to hand. Clearly similar forgeries were being made here. And from where did these people obtain the ideas used for these dilutions? I swore to myself that I would by no means provide them with any of my verses, which otherwise could very easily happen. Perhaps they would cook up a watery soup from them.— Meanwhile, my gaze wandered further over the curiosities on the floor. My heart lifted when I saw there, amidst a great deal of rubbish, pure poetic words, profound symbols, adages of lofty wisdom shining forth.

"Whoever brings order to this," I exclaimed enthusiastically, "would find the makings of the most wonderful poetry. Give me the clutter and I won't begrudge you a bit of the effort!"

The smugglers declared themselves willing.

Meanwhile, we had become hungry again. We dined together in the square cave. At the table I learned remarkable details about the existence of these people. They lived by barter. It had begun in a small way. They had found some valuables on the path. They had increased their holdings through favorable exchanges. More and more I gathered the impression that not all of these exchanges were conducted honestly.

"Will you also leave something behind for us, in exchange for our gifts?" they asked me.

I was alarmed; I had nothing with me other than a rather lousy German poet's cigar.

"Don't worry; leave us three of your dreams and we will be satisfied."

"Dreams?" I cried, with a sigh. "I have plenty of those. If you know a way I can painlessly rid myself of a few ..."

We then moved on to other topics of conversation, to politics, to the prevalent dissatisfaction of the people with their rulers. The smugglers acted as if they had had a hand in this in some way.

"No, no, no," one of them exclaimed. "We'll not return the true revolution again so soon. It took a great deal of effort to get it back in exchange for hypocrisy, which is a high price. Almost daily we receive letters from France; they would like us to give it back, and in return they will deliver the glory of Bonaparte undiminished. But we will not do it. At most they'll get some street fighting." (I note here that the year '48 was fast approaching.)

A dry laugh, revolting beyond measure, rang out from the corner. Bones had erupted in merriment.

"Big mouths, all of you," cried the old woman. "You will have to surrender anyway, when Lady Fate comes and demands it. Heh . . . heh . . . Good thing she watches over you, otherwise you would have turned the whole world upside down. Heh . . . heh . . ."

The smuggler who had spoken earlier seized hold of a rope that the old woman always wore around her left ankle and hung her head-down on a high nail that projected from the face of the rock. She whimpered a little, but appeared to be accustomed to this kind of well-deserved punishment. The five hundred women, whose door still stood open, began shouting. The one lying closest to us said, with a slight foreign accent, that she would never stand for such a thing. But one would hardly have tried such a thing with her. She had a regal form.

I became ever more confirmed in my poor opinion of these people. They appeared to be authorities on authenticity and knew how to place it among their holdings in order to debase it. Of course they did good business, frittering the great revolution in numberless street battles that they peddled individually. I could imagine how many thoughtful ideas and honorable sentiments they took for such trifles, and it dawned on me how the business of these men depended on such dishonest dealings. A frightening thought arose in me: if they busied themselves in this same way for some time they eventually will have pulled everything worthwhile out of the world and smuggled in their own illusory values and dilutions. I shuddered at the thought of the cowardice, hypocrisy, falsehood, and oppression that would then prevail, while freedom, beauty, knowledge moldered in rock chambers as curiosities or alchemical distortions. It was just as well that they were at least afraid of fate, perhaps because it is the one thing in the world which you can't trade in.

They must have poured something soporific into my drink, because it was only with great difficulty that I observed, as Bones was once again set on her feet, a boiling cauldron brought out of the opening of a tunnel and moved to the center which, amidst a hellish din, was stirred by the entire smuggler gang. They threw in unrecognizable objects; bottles were emptied into it. When the cauldron was too full they simply tipped it until some of the fluid ran over and, like creeping worms, spread silent and thick into the tunnels. Then it was further watered down. Lastly, the old woman glued a label with the date of the following day on the kettle, which several smugglers then sealed. They pushed it over to an iron door. Through the opening I saw nothing but the starry sky. I realized that we must be quite high up. The kettle was pushed to the threshold. Bones gave it a kick and it rolled on a kind of chute down into the valley. The entire gang of smugglers howled the crudest expressions after it, spat down and defiled even the chute with their foul mouths.

"It's burst!" one of them cried excitedly, and I vividly pictured how this miserable brew would inundate the world the next morning. Evidently there was such a serving sent every day.

Now, their purpose apparently achieved, they closed the door. However, I acted as if I were still asleep, because, as I didn't hide from myself, I acknowledged that I had fallen in with an unusual circle, one whose activities I wanted to observe further. But, however much I fought against it, I soon found myself in a half doze. I had vivid dreams, all the while knowing that they were dreams.

First, I saw Manolitha, divinely beautiful, as she lived in my imagination, with her crown of golden hair and stars in her eyes. I knew it was just an image in a dream, but I was glad to see her. But then one of the smugglers came, reached for something over Manolitha's head, carefully rolled up the entire image and handed it to the old woman, who carried it into one of the tunnels. In place of the image I saw a peculiar front door with green blinds. Over the door hung a transparent illuminated house number the size of a windowpane. Next to that, between two crude cupids, was a sign that read:

Night Bell for
Mlle. Rose, Modes.

I was bold enough to ring the bell. There behind the blinds I saw two peering eyes. The door opened a crack and a very modestly dressed girl with a slightly pockmarked face whispered, "You were referred . . . by Dr. M., were you not? . . . As you know, we only accept referrals . . ."

I just nodded, and went in. At the end of the corridor I again looked into the half-open red chamber where the five hundred naked women were encamped. They now belonged to me, but the door slammed shut all the same.

The modest girl pushed me onto a broad, elaborate wooden staircase, like those found in respectable old houses. I went up. It smelled of Saturday cleaning. On the fourth floor was a glass door, next to which I found my name on a small sign. I opened it with my house key, which fit the lock exactly. In the room was a set coffee table, by which, in the glow of a floral kerosene lamp, Manolitha was knitting socks. Behind the table was a leather sofa with a crocheted, wreath-shaped pillow. Over it hung family portraits in oval frames. Manolitha stood up. She looked very good as a housewife.

"It's a good thing that you've come, old chap," she said. "The butcher has already been here three times with his bill . . ."

I wanted to approach her and kiss the part in her hair, but the smuggler came back, busied himself above Manolitha's head and rolled up the entire dream image, and the old woman once again carried it into the tunnel. Instead of an old-fashioned room with the smell of coffee, I found myself in a small chamber full of oriental carpets on the floor and on the walls. A servant was awaiting me with tea. Next to my cup lay a pile of letters and telegrams, which I reached for while the servant took off my boots. Countless candles burned in front of mirrors in the next room. In the middle of the room was a table set with opulent silver and porcelain; from colorful vases came the scent of rare blooms. The servant deferentially remarked that everything was set for dinner, as I had ordered. At that moment the bell rang: I was called to the telephone.

But as I put the receiver to my ear I noticed that I had a peep show in front of me. Inside it I saw a wonderful image. Deep in the depths a river wound between lushly overgrown Mediterranean banks, where an almost black laurel grove stood out from the lighter green. Out of this grove arose a form that floated higher and higher, until it was right in front of me. I recognized Manolitha's features, as beautiful as they lived in me. She wore an antique gown. She solemnly approached me, raised her arms and was about to press a laurel wreath into my temples when, for the third time, the smuggler appeared, rolled up the image and gave it to Bones, who disappeared with it into the tunnel. In the peep show, however, I was granted another spectacle. A gentleman, who resembled my father, only far more distinguished, was addressing a festive gathering from a platform. They were cheering him; he appeared to have just finished his speech. I managed to hear him say: "And for this booklet, in which I portrayed his country in the truest and at the same time the brightest colors, His Highness the Bey of Tunis awarded me his Order of the Sun. My sovereign—may God preserve him—for secret state reasons, could not permit me to wear this award, and so I feel compelled to return this evidence of the favor of the High Bey—may God preserve him, as well. But before I do, I cannot deny myself the satisfaction, revered listeners and—how I do flatter myself—friends, the satisfaction of seeing this gem."

With these words the distinguished man opened a box, which was brought to him by the same servant who had earlier served me tea and had pulled off my boots. The man took from it a golden star with silk ribbons, which he showed to the loudly cheering crowd. He simply could not keep himself from putting it on for a moment.

At that moment the telephone rang again. Someone shouted, "Stop!" I hung up the receiver and as I looked around I saw that it was now bright morning. The smugglers were having a meal in their rock parlor.

They wished me good day and Bones brought an entirely tolerable morning coffee to my couch. I learned that the smugglers intended to go about their day's work after breakfast—that is, they wanted to make a few forays into the surrounding country, because today Prince Metternich, understood to be on his way to Italy, was going to pass through and they wanted to trick him into buying some liberal ideas. They hoped by using such manipulations they would not have to give back the revolution. They set off, and for me nothing remained but to go along. The smugglers noticed my disappointment.

"Oh yes, about the gifts," one of them said, "you should know that you won't be receiving them all at once. They will be spread out across your entire lifetime. But this very day you will still find that we keep our word."

Naturally I didn't believe a word, and was convinced that they had cheated me.

We went through a seemingly endless tunnel which in the end led us to a part of the lake where there was no path between water and cliff. A wide cargo boat, the kind boatmen use, was moored in a small natural bay. I was rowed for half an hour and dropped off on the quayside I knew. The smugglers waited not even a full minute before heading back at an incredible speed.

Without being in the least clear about my experience, I went into the town. From a distance I saw Manolitha, who was coming from the market where she had bought fish. She carried them in a basket. Phoo! How ugly she was. She seemed to me to be morbidly thin, and how her hands must have reeked of fish! Fortunately, the path led over a bridge, under which I reached a ditch that ran beside the road. I hid there until Manolitha had passed. I have never seen her again.

When I arrived at the town's market square I found that a large crowd had gathered in front of the most elegant inn. They were being restrained by footmen in livery. Among those leaving the inn I thought I noticed one of the smugglers. He immediately disappeared into the crowd. Upon inquiring, I learned from my neighbor that a high personage who was passing through on the way to Italy had arrived. No one knew who it was, because the personage wanted to remain anonymous. I immediately knew that it could be none other than Prince Metternich. With a finesse otherwise out of character for me, I managed to sneak into the house through the garden in the back. I, who am normally rather shy, stood so unabashedly before a jib door that everyone who passed by believed that I belonged there. Through the door I heard

the voice of the prince in conversation with the mayor of the town. I could only make out fragments of sentences. Above all, he wished to travel through unrecognized, because he was ill. Otherwise, he was very well disposed toward the town. He had no objection to the appointment of the popular X as postmaster, although the man had a reputation as a liberal. One should not at all take him (the prince) to be some kind of werewolf: he also intended, over the course of years, to be somewhat more moderate with censorship and laws regarding the press, even in the border districts, etc., etc.

When I heard the mayor making his farewell, I hurried away to avoid detection. My path led me straight to the editor of the town's top newspaper, where I revealed everything I knew.

"Metternich here?" cried the editor. "If you are trying to fool me . . ."

"But, sir," I replied, "what do you take me for? I know Prince Metternich's voice as well as I do my own father's."

I shocked myself with this inexplicable audacity because I had never seen Metternich, had never before heard him speak.

"Well, write down everything that you know," the editor replied, persuaded by my certainty. "Here is a desk, ink, and pen . . ."

While I was writing, images and phrases I had noticed in the smugglers' prison flowed into me—I didn't know how. In a quarter of an hour two columns were written in an extremely brilliant style, as I myself thought. With great confidence I handed the editor the pages. He scanned them and cried out in surprise. "You are a born journalist, young man . . . Your cleverness is as nothing compared to your style, and both are surpassed by your speed. How long have you been working in the press?"

"This is my first article," I replied, somewhat shyly.

"What were you before? Every journalist used to be something else."

"Poet," I said, embarrassed.

"Well, it's a good thing you gave that up. Rubini will be singing *Cenerontola* this evening. Go to the opera and bring me your review tonight."

"But, sir, I am quite unmusical."

"Nonsense," he answered, gruffly. "Rid yourself of any such doubts. With your style you can be musical, agronomic, geographic, theosophical . . . Whatever is required . . . Do you understand? I see, by the way, that you will need to freshen your appearance if you are to go to the opera. Here is a hundred guilders advance for you; sign this paper."

He handed me slip of paper, which I signed without reading. I took my leave and went to a haberdashery where I outfitted myself from head to toe. I came home a dandy. At the door to my room stood a pompous, excessively elegantly dressed lady.

"Oh . . . you have finally arrived . . . ," she exclaimed in broken German. "I am Rubini . . . Carlotta Rubini . . . I hear that you will write review tonight."

I was a little flustered with embarrassment.

"Forgive me . . . Signora . . ." I stammered . . . "I am only living in this hole temporarily . . . until I find an apartment to my taste."

"Oh, I understand . . . I understand . . . ," said Rubini, and she entered.

She took off her veil and I recognized her as the one of the five hundred women who had lain closest to me in the smugglers' lair.

"Oh . . . I am so tired . . . ," she said. "May I rest a little . . . I stand on stairs for half an hour."

"Certainly . . . Certainly . . . Signora, if only I could offer you something . . ."

"Oh, yes, sir . . . , offer something . . . , get me something."

I went out and gave the cobbler's lad next door the rest of my money and instructed him to bring champagne from the café. So I had to admit that the smugglers had kept their word, and would be sending me the five hundred women as well as the essential million piece by piece.

When I went back into the room, Rubini had made herself very comfortable. She was so hot. And when the champagne came, I was already holding her

hand, concerned, because she had an excessively strong
heartbeat . . .

But she only set a precedent. I could go on to tell another
four hundred and ninety-nine stories if the high birth,
the European titles, and the wealth of my heroines did
not obligate me to an exceptional discretion. But perhaps at some point, out of purely psychological interest,
I will once again be indiscreet. I only have to wait for
some dynasties to die off.

THE ACTIVE INGREDIENTS OF *HASHISH*
DECADENCE, DIABOLISM, AND DE SADE

For Oscar A. H. Schmitz, the refined, neurasthenic swoon of the fin-de-siècle coincided with a period of personal crisis. The high-tension ringing of the German writer's nerves harmonized with the coda of the dying nineteenth century—an unease, an enervation, a longing for renewal that he shared with many of his contemporaries. But for a dandified cosmopolite like Schmitz there was also allure in decline, in the arcane rites and lurid conjunctions picked out by the rays of the setting sun. "We were decadent, and we chose to be," said Schmitz of this era, having traced the source of this sensibility back to its spiritual home: France. All of this fed into the tales of sacrilege, lust, and terror that made up his 1902 book *Hashish*. Not just a conduit of French literary modes, it was also Germany's first major example of drug writing and a precursor to the twentieth-century boom in macabre fiction.

In 1897 Schmitz was in his mid-twenties, freshly orphaned, with little more than a respectable inheritance and some derivative poetry to his name. He abandoned his studies and spent much of the year in Paris. Francophile by inclination, he avidly consumed the pleasures, novelties, and curiosities the Belle Époque had to offer. He detailed his wandering days and wassailing nights in a diary, although one searches in vain for mention of major events that coincided with his stay, such as the fire at the Bazar de la Charité—a tragedy that dominated headlines around the world.

Instead, Schmitz's diary is an inward-looking account. It records, for example, his frequent visits to the long-running Tuesday salon hosted by the provocateuse Rachilde, author of such transgressive works as *The Marquise de Sade*. Other attendees included seasoned debauchee Jean Lorrain and a young Alfred Jarry, whose *Ubu Roi* had recently exploded onto the Paris stage. These were Schmitz's tutors in the school for scandal, and he heeded their lessons well. This was an environment still imbued with the rare and heady perfume of Decadence, which—beginning with J. K. Huysmans and his 1884 novel *À rebours*—had proposed an alternative to the earthy pieties of Naturalism by celebrating perversity, artifice, and arch individuality.

Schmitz encountered both Aubrey Beardsley and Lord Alfred Douglas at Rachilde's salon, and reported a brief exchange that could scarcely be improved upon as an example of fin-de-siècle ennui (Schmitz: "*La vie anglaise est bien triste n'est-ce pas*?" Douglas: "*La vie est triste partout*"). Schmitz later claimed to have glimpsed a bedraggled Oscar Wilde there "on an autumn day," but here we must question his account. Wilde's sole visit to Paris in 1897 occurred in late September, a time when, according to his own diary, Schmitz was vacationing on the Normandy coast, and so it appears unlikely that the two Oscars were ever in the same room together. That Schmitz might have wished it so is significant enough.

Schmitz was infected by the vivid curiosity for mysticism, spiritualism, and even Satanism afoot in 1890s Paris. He attended a Martinist ritual, familiarized himself with occult writers such as Eliphas Levi and Stanislas de Guaita, and visited the Rose+Croix exhibition hosted by Joséphin Péladan, the "sandwich man of the beyond" responsible for the modern Rosicrucian revival. We also know from Schmitz's diaries that he tried hashish on at least one occasion in Paris, during which he played the piano for hours—"better," he claimed, "than ever before."

But there was a mental cost attached to these bacchanalian excesses, and Schmitz suffered from a nervous complaint which appears to have inspired a turning point—what we might now term a quarter-life crisis. "More and more I come to realize what a failure I've been so far in life," he confided to his diary at the time. With weak nerves and poor physical health, he experienced a first dawning awareness of his mortality and the limits of his earthly powers, a realization he described as a "memento mori."

Following the 1898 publication of his first book, a volume of verse entitled *Orpheus* which owed a heavy debt to German poet Stefan George, the dawn of the new century found Schmitz processing his Parisian experience in pieces that would later become *Hashish*. He was encouraged by praise for the work-in-progress from his friend, Jugendstil architect August Endell (who was shortly to marry Schmitz's former lover Else Plötz, later notorious as the "Dada Baroness," Elsa von Freytag-Loringhoven). Plagued anew by emotional disturbance, Schmitz took to a sanatorium in 1900, where he met an Austrian banker who was similarly impressed by Schmitz's twisted tales. They were, in fact, close in theme and atmosphere to pieces the Austrian himself was working on, and Schmitz assisted him in getting them published, thus helping to launch the author we now know as Gustav Meyrink.

Finally, the seeds planted in that formative Parisian trip of 1897 broke through the topsoil in 1902 when Südwestdeutscher

Verlag, a small Frankfurt publishing house, issued Schmitz's first book of prose: *Haschisch*. Apart from the setting, numerous influences absorbed during this period of experimentation make their way into the text. Here the titular drug isn't just a portal to altered consciousness; it also serves to blast open narrative potential. Moreover, it explicitly signals the author's emulation of (predominantly French) exponents of drug writing, including Théophile Gautier and Charles Baudelaire. The latter's *Les paradis artificiels* (1860) in particular established a thematic association between hashish and Satanism that greatly influenced Schmitz's work.

This gesture of *hommage* also represented Germany's first book-length contribution to drug literature. The country's writers had waited far longer to explore pharmacological enchantments than the aforementioned French writers or their Anglophone counterparts (Coleridge, de Quincey, Poe, Ludlow). In 1890, for instance, German writer Isolde Kurz published the curtly titled "Haschisch." As well as the title, her short story shares with Schmitz's tales the time-traveling illusions of its stoned protagonist. In 1897 came a German opera of the same name, an orientalist fantasy. Schmitz, an opera enthusiast, may well have seen it or at least been aware of the work, although his diary makes no mention of it.

Of the numerous French influences on Schmitz's work, Huysmans looms largest, particularly his novels *À rebours* (1884) and *Là-Bas* (1891). In fact, with its demonic raptures and subsequent remorse, Schmitz's slim volume is almost a fast-forward replay of Huysmans's initial attraction to and ultimate rejection of Satanism, perversity, and the macabre, an arc which in the French author's case took several novels to relate. *Hashish* is steeped—to the point of parody, or postmodernism—in the French Decadence of which

Huysmans was the undisputed paragon. Sex, in the world of *Hashish*, is inseparable from death, served together on a bed of overripe Catholicism. The synesthesia experienced by the protagonist is not just an effect of the drug but a distinguishing device of Decadent prose. Blasphemy, artifice, disease, diabolism, and ennui; ruins, rare jewels, hothouses, exotic blooms, and cruel women—almost the entire litany of Decadent motifs is present.

The breakdown and ensuing breakthrough that the poet achieves in the six stories of *Hashish* (and, for that matter, in "Smugglers' Pass") parallel Schmitz's Parisian experience. The first story in the cycle, "The Hashish Club," is clearly inspired by Gautier's *Club des Hachichins* (1846)—which describes the palatial Ile Saint-Louis drug lair that he frequented—as well as Baudelaire's treatment of the same theme. We are guided by the unnamed narrator, a "German poet"; there can be no doubt that he is a stand-in for Schmitz himself. The writer slips a meta-moment in among his numerous other appropriations by crediting the protagonist with his own poem "Galathea," included in the *Orpheus* collection.

It is an old acquaintance, "aging dandy" Count Vittorio Alta-Carrara, who quotes this verse when he meets the narrator by chance in a Paris restaurant. The name bears a glancing resemblance to that of Daucus-Carota, the mysterious moderator of the author's hallucinations in *Club des Hachichins*. But might the count actually have been modeled on Gabriele d'Annunzio? True, the Italian Decadent writer differed physically from the description of Alta-Carrara, and wasn't ennobled until 1924. But d'Annunzio was an unquestionably dandyish figure of aristocratic mien. Schmitz was certainly aware of him; he attended one of the writer's plays—starring the Italian's lover, Eleonora Duse—during his Paris stay. And there's another intriguing clue. In the text the narrator mentions his first encounter with Alta-Carrara in a Roman salon, where they had taken tea in the company of statues. This scenario corresponds with his 1898 visit to a salon in the Palazzo Zuccari, overlooking the Spanish Steps, where guests gathered "amid ancient statues and Renaissance paintings," as his diary relates. This location has a particularly strong association with d'Annunzio, who regularly visited and included it as a setting in his first novel, *Piacere* (*Pleasure*), published in 1889. The palazzo's Mannerist exterior, incidentally, features a doorway in the shape of a demonic face, grotesquely distended.

The name Count Alta-Carrara points to another possible reference. In his 1884 novel *Le vice suprême*, Joséphin Péladan declares that "perversity is the aristocracy of evil" and offers numerous touchpoints—Sinistrari, Semiramis, Don Juan, Baudelaire, de Sade, Venice, dogaressas—that later appear in *Hashish*, along with a Parisian backdrop. But just as significantly, *Le vice suprême* features a certain Count Alta. Later, the physical description of the hashish-club patron whose story forms "The Sin against the Holy Ghost" closely matches the best-known portrait of Péladan, painted in 1891 by Alexandre Séon.

The inspiration for "The Devil's Lover" is straightforward enough—a report about an anonymous assignation related by a composer friend that Schmitz recorded in his diary. To this Schmitz adds mystical embellishments, a sprinkle of modish Satanism, and some local color acquired on a trip to Jersey in the summer of 1897; as the story reflects, he was particularly appalled by the islanders' diet. At another point in his diaries, Schmitz recollects an all-night Parisian carousal with a friend from Munich. Toward dawn the pair wandered through the Marais, where Schmitz marveled at the *hôtels particuliers* and their "sumptuous architectonic forms." This may well have been when the inspiration for the story "A Night in the Eighteenth Century" first struck.

This "night" is precisely defined as 15 September 1768. The annals reveal no event of particular note on that date in Paris, which is not to say that it is not significant. The key figure of the Count of Saint-Germain (ca. 1712–1784) here doubles as Gilles de Rais (a.k.a. Gilles de Montmorency-Laval, Baron de Rais, here Gilles de Laval), the medieval child murderer who features prominently in Huysmans's *Là-Bas*. The account of barbarous aristocratic caprice in a pre-Revolutionary French setting—complete with violent aphrodisiac—naturally also evokes another nobleman, the Marquis de Sade. The date of Gilles de Rais's arrest was 15 September 1440, and Sade was first arrested in the year 1768; combine them and you have the date in question.

Like the shape-shifting Alta-Carrara, with whom he merges personae, there is much uncertainty about the Count of Saint-Germain. He moved about the courts of Louis XV and other European rulers in the mid-eighteenth century and claimed to be of Transylvanian royal blood. Casanova, though charmed by him, spoke of "his boastings, his barefaced lies, and his manifold eccentricities"; Saint-Germain's claim of having lived for hundreds of years arguably belongs to all three categories.

Literary scholar Uwe Schütte points to a contemporary text that also features a Parisian setting and a precise timestamp that may have influenced Schmitz—Arthur Schnitzler's 1899 one-act play *Der grüne Kakadu* (The green cockatoo). The narrative of Schnitzler's grotesque unfolds on the fateful day of 14 July 1789, and finds down-at-heel actors meeting in the eponymous tavern where they are joined by a group of slumming aristocrats, hoping—much like Schmitz's jaded nobility—for a piquant encounter with their social inferiors; all are overtaken by the revolution, which is repeatedly foreshadowed in Schmitz's story.

In "Carnival" the action shifts to Venice, the Decadent location *non pareil*. Here the primary influence appears to be Edgar Allan Poe (see "The Assignation," or "Ligeia"). Decades after Schmitz's hashish experience, Walter Benjamin reported a "Satanic phase" in his own experiments with the drug, noting "the feeling that I understood Poe better." Here Schmitz assumes his place in a grand lineage starting with the Gothic novel and advancing through E. T. A. Hoffmann, Poe, Jules Barbey d'Aurevilly, and Vernon Lee, and continuing after Schmitz to early twentieth-century champions of macabre, fantastical literature such as Meyrink, Karl Hans Strobl, Hanns Heinz Ewers, H. P. Lovecraft, and reaching to Thomas Ligotti in the present day.

Huysmans returns in "The Sin against the Holy Ghost." The frenzied climax of the story takes the form of a profane, ecstatic dance; anyone familiar with *À rebours* will recognize similarities with that book's description of Gustave Moreau's painting of Salome. The black masses of *La-Bàs* also figure heavily. The methodical corruption of virtue as a diversion practiced by the debauched idle rich, the tale's narrative engine, recalls Pierre Choderlos de Laclos's 1782 epistolary novel *Les liaisons dangereuses*. Uwe Schütte sees a parallel with Heinrich von Kleist's short story "Die heilige Cäcilie" (1810), another mystical tale of sacrilege thwarted. Schmitz himself declared that the story evolved during long talks on the subject of Catholic mysticism with a certain Père Thomas (Schmitz himself almost "came out to Rome" but backed out of conversion at the last minute). How the good father felt about effectively sharing his name with the story's Satanic padre, Friar Tomás, is a matter of conjecture.

In "The Message," the narrator is accosted by an insistent prostitute at the moment when his inchoate doubts are swelling into a crisis of purpose. This, again, appears to have been inspired by a Parisian encounter. In March 1897 Schmitz confided an "abomination" to his diary, an old streetwalker who approached the writer on Boulevard Sébastopol, offering her wares with the assurance that she was "*très cochonne*." The desolation overwhelming the narrator finds its metaphor; for the arrogant young buck about town, an aging prostitute may indeed have been the very embodiment of futility. That she is also (or the narrator believes her to be) an incubus, or death incarnate, unites the theme of personal calamity with the book's more outlandish motifs. The young protagonist sees his existence stripped of illusion, a moment of clarity in which he realizes that his way of life must change. Here, beneath the ennui and the Gallic Decadent tropes, lurk weltschmerz and the ur-Germanic form of the *bildungsroman*. It's a form that also underpins the strange appendage, "Smugglers' Pass." This work, with its wish fulfillment, fairy-tale conventions, and labored metaphors, is not at first glance a logical fit with the *Hashish* cycle. But just as in the larger work, here an unnamed German poet (again, Schmitz himself) reaches a crossroads in his early adult life. In fact the story can be viewed as an idealized response to the question dangling at the end of *Hashish*—"what to do with this new lease on life?"

The German literary milieu into which *Hashish* was propelled was aware of Decadence, as a fashionable affectation if nothing else. It was a vogue embraced by those who, as writer and agitator Erich Mühsam put it, "slept with a book by Oscar Wilde under their pillows and entered the café with another by Stefan George under their arms and an opium cigarette in their mouths." His unflattering description continued: "The great fashion was for aestheticism, for fatigue, for absinthe, for morphine, for pallor, a blasé attitude, and all manner of romantic anomalies . . . Anemia was considered ethereal and one wore orchids as a symbol of morbid decadence."[1]

For all its fashionable horrors and outrageous vices, *Hashish* attracted little attention at first, although there were positive notices. Stefan Zweig found it a "late-born child of that Satanic literature in France . . . which, buoyantly and downright ingeniously imaginative as it is, conforms with remarkable fidelity to the refined, cool style of Poe, Hoffmann, Baudelaire and Barbey d'Aurevilly." The Austrian writer praised it as "one of the most distinctive and stylistically exceptional novella books of recent years."[2]

Following its first publication in 1902, *Hashish* went into a number of editions, and later Schmitz would say, "I may flatter myself that I introduced a new literary genre in Germany, the modern, fantastical story," adding: "Back then no one knew the names Meyrink and Ewers."[3] But significantly, Schmitz makes no particular claim for *Hashish* as a Decadent work, perhaps because doing so would have burdened it with a label that by then had become decidedly démodé. Even as fin-de-siècle writers and artists underwent reevaluation in the second half of the twentieth century, with an expanded focus on European works beyond the French origins of Decadence, Schmitz was barely mentioned. *Hashish* remains a puzzling omission from almost every major study of Decadent literary works from Germany. Even a cursory reading confirms that it deserves to be counted among their number.

James J. Conway

THE ACTIVE INGREDIENTS OF HASHISH

NOTES

1. Erich Mühsam, *Unpolitische Erinnerungen* (Leipzig: Offizin Haag-Drugulin, 1931).

2. Stefan Zweig, "Skizzen- und Novellenbücher," in: *Das litterarische Echo* 5 (1902/03).

3. Oscar A. H. Schmitz, *Dämon Welt* (Munich: Georg Müller, 1926).

Alfred Kubin (1877–1959) was an Austrian graphic artist and illustrator whose work had ties to the *Blaue Reiter* group, Symbolism, and Expressionism. He was also an author of several books, his best known the dark fantasy novel *The Other Side* (1909). The many authors he illustrated included Edgar Allan Poe, E. T. A. Hoffmann, Dostoyevsky, Mynona, and his brother-in-law, Oscar A. H. Schmitz.

W. C. Bamberger has translated works by Gershom Scholem, Emil Szittya, and Hermann Finsterlin, among others. Recent essays have addressed subjects ranging from Wonder Woman comics to the language of poet Anne Carson to the critical reception of Ray Bradbury. His most recent novel is *A Light Like Ida Lupino*. He lives in Michigan.

James J. Conway is an Australian-born writer and translator based in Berlin, and the creator of Strange Flowers, an online repository of alternative cultural history. In 2017 he founded Rixdorf Editions, launching the small press with his own translations of historic texts by Franziska zu Reventlow and Magnus Hirschfeld.